# Valentino's Hair

# *Valentino's Hair*

## BY YVONNE V. SAPIA

*Winner of the 1991*
*Nilon Award*

FICTION
COLLECTIVE
TWO
Boulder • Normal

This book is the winner of the 1991 Charles H. and N.
Mildred Nilon Excellence in Minority Fiction Award,
sponsored by the University of Colorado and Fiction
Collective Two

Published jointly by the University of Colorado at
Boulder, and Fiction Collective Two with assistance from
the National Endowment for the Arts, the support of the
Publications Center, University of Colorado at Boulder,
and the cooperation of Illinois State University, Normal,
and the Teachers & Writers Collaborative.

Address all inquiries to: Fiction Collective Two, English
Department Publications Center, University of Colorado at
Boulder, Boulder CO 80309-0494.

*Valentino's Hair*
  Yvonne V. Sapia

Cloth, ISBN:  0-932511-45-7
Paper, ISBN:  0-932511-46-5


Distributed by the Talman Company
Typesetting and Design - Carol Friedman and Gail Gaboda

ઢ

Grateful acknowledgement is made to the editors of
*Apalachee Quarterly, Cincinnati Poetry Review, Indiana
Review, Kalliope,* and *The Reaper* for publishing previous
versions of portions of this novel. Appreciation is also
extended to Northeastern University Press for the publica-
tion of an early version of the first chapter, "His Father
Cannot Help But Tell." Special thanks is conveyed to the
Florida State University Department of English for the
generous support a fellowship provided during the comple-
tion of *Valentino's Hair.* And a humble thank you to
Facundo Sapia, the barber who actually cut Rudolph
Valentino's hair and bestowed upon his daughter a valuable legacy.

# TABLE OF CONTENTS

*Chapter One*

## HIS FATHER CANNOT HELP BUT TELL

It's been almost thirty-five years. I can scarcely believe it, *niño*. Time trusts no one and so it disappears before us like the smoke, the smoke from my cigarette. In 1926 I was young, and I was a part of a world filled with such life, a world which was eating at its own edges without being satisfied. The Roaring Twenties—they didn't roar, Lupe. They swelled with passions. They danced, and I danced with them.

I had a barber shop in a magnificent hotel in Manhattan. Unfortunately, it is not there anymore. It burned down during World War II. But in its time it was elegant and very private. My shop was small, only one chair, and not in any way the size of my shop here. But my barber shop in the hotel . . . it was a special place. Every comb, every lotion, every towel was perfect, like the stars you love which burn in the dark sky. Everything gleamed. The barber chair was gold-leafed and made of the softest leather. A man could fall asleep in that chair with lather still fresh on his face. There were four large oval mirrors, two on one wall, two on the opposite wall. I always thought they stared at each other like distant lovers, never permitted to kiss, only allowed to long for each other with their cool but secretive stares.

Oh, and the walls, the walls had wallpaper which was like cloth. The wallpaper too had gold leaf with a blue and brown background of leaves and trees and ocean in the distance. And it reminded me of Aguadilla, the great stretches of beach and the lush rain forests of Puerto Rico.

Anyway, fate had been good to me, and I was owner of the barber shop in the hotel, and I made good money, and the times looked good, and I lost a lot of money before the Twenties were gone.

But that's not why I'm telling you all of this.

One day in 1926, it was the early afternoon around 1:00 p.m., things were slow, and I was reading the paper and studying the horse racing sheet. Mangual had come by and picked up a couple of bets from me and got a haircut. (He had hair in those days.) It was just after he had left, and I remember thinking about what a hot summer we were having, and I was tipped back in my barber chair almost sleeping, almost dreaming. You know how it is when you're between sleep and dream, and a slight push can send you into one world or the other.

Well, suddenly the wall phone rang. I thought for sure it was Mangual. Sometimes he'd call and try to get me to change my bets. He'd tell me I was wasting my money, and he had a tip on a horse he'd swear was so fast you'd think it had six legs.

The phone rang a second time. I did not hurry. I don't quite know why, but I waited until the fourth ring and snapped forward in the chair and lifted the phone receiver off the hook. The front desk at the hotel was calling. A guest wanted a haircut and a shave immediately. Of course, since I had no customers in the shop, no one except maybe one or two flies searching for decay in the summer heat, I said I was available and asked for the room number. That was that. Just another customer, I remember thinking. Possibly a rich stockbroker, a businessman, maybe Mafia. I'd given them haircuts and shaves too.

I took my best tools. I had recently purchased them and had a special black leather box made. Like a doctor. In a way I felt I was a kind of doctor. What I did helped people ride a stream to slow recovery, to arrive on the shore of something new, something which was hidden from sight. A secret place. A secret person.

Well, so I went. I closed my shop, putting a note on the door saying I'd be back in an hour, and then I walked down the wine-red carpeted hallway into the lobby, past the front desk and into the elevator. I pressed the button for the eighth floor and rode up alone to my destiny. There was a small mirror on the elevator wall, just above the button panel. I guess it was there for the ladies and gentlemen, on their way to parties, to look one last time at the present. And so I did. I stared into the face of a twenty-seven-year-old man who knew so little about the ways of this world. And for that moment I thought I saw someone else. Someone who was walking towards me from another place we held in common. The elevator door opened and seemed to wake me from my daydream.

Room 808 was my customer, and I found myself at the door tapping lightly on its face. Room 808 was one of the larger suites. The rooms were spacious, and the windows faced Central Park. I could hear the sound of an electric fan as the door opened, and I was greeted by a fair-haired and frail-looking young man. He was in a dark suit, and he was smoking a cigarette in a cigarette holder. Quite a dandy. He greeted me warmly, thanking me for being so prompt. His employer was absolutely desperate to be ready for an evening engagement and had little time or desire to walk the busy streets looking for a barber shop, and if he did walk the streets, he probably would be mobbed by admirers, and he would

definitely make my time worthwhile, and I had come
highly recommended.

Well, all these things came quickly out of this
amiable, high-strung American as he led me to a room
where the light was good and which had been prepared
with a chair, table, and large mirror. The sink was to the
left of the table. I began setting the tools on the table and
emptying my satchel of hair and skin products, which I
had also brought with me. As I did, I looked up at the
mirror, but more to see if it was clean than anything else.
When I did, in the mirror I saw the reflection of a dark-
haired man who was standing in the doorway behind me.
It was the man you saw in the silent film we watched
together. It was Rudolph Valentino. He looked drawn
and tired. He had obviously not shaved, for his face was
already darkening with whiskers. He was wearing a very
white undershirt and a pair of dark pants. By his side was
a very slim and exotic-looking woman. They were arguing,
but very quietly, in whispers like lovers separated by a
thin wall from their neighbors. The woman kept insisting
on something, and she called him Rudy. He finally looked
at me staring at him in the mirror and smiled slightly and
stopped the woman in her sentence by simply saying,
"Enough!" and telling her they'd talk later. He closed the
door behind him and walked towards me with his hand
out to shake my hand.

And to my surprise he said my name. He said
something like, "I'm glad to meet you, Señor Nieves." The
look of amazement must have been all over my face. I
suddenly began to feel flushed, and I could see how red
my cheeks were in the mirror. And then he apologized
and told me that his secretary had a bad habit of never
informing people who their customer was. One time in
California, he said, he needed a manicure and a pedicure.

The hotel sent up an elderly lady to give him what he requested. But she was never told who her client was. When Valentino walked out to greet her, he had his pants legs rolled up, and he was barefoot. The woman drew in a long hard look and fainted on the royal blue rug, her silver hair perfectly in place, and Valentino tried to revive her and members of his party called for the house doctor and all was panic. And the strange thing was that they couldn't revive her. They declared the woman dead within the half hour, Valentino concluded, remorse clearly in his voice. He went on to say that the hotel cooperated and reported the woman died of a heart attack out in the hallway and not in Valentino's room. He had enough of scandal. This would have been too cruel, too bizarre, he confessed. I was struck dumb by Valentino's story. Why should he tell me, Facundo Nieves, a mere barber?

Lupe, I was suddenly caught between laughing and crying. The poor man had a power he couldn't control, and here I was absolving him of his sin, listening to his confession like a priest in my white smock. And now he was to do penance, he was to give something up to me. I would raise my chalice of shaving cream and lift my silver razor to the light and strip away the veil.

He said my name again. "Nieves means snow, doesn't it?" "Yes," I told him. "My mother's name was Inocencia." "Ah," he said, "what a beautiful name, Innocent Snow." And he sat down in the chair and looked into the mirror and then asked me to help him with this man in the mirror, meaning, of course, himself. I covered him with the white apron. And I began to apply the shaving cream to his face while his eyes stared directly into the eyes of the pitiful man he thought he saw in the mirror. I began to lather and disguise that perfect face, slowly, with compliance, like an accomplice to the development of the belief in one god. Perhaps her god was what the elderly lady thought she saw before she fainted into death. I don't know.

As I shaved Rudolph Valentino, he remained silent, and I remained silent. My hands had to be steady, for they guided the instrument and I simply followed. For some reason Valentino noticed my hands. He said they looked like his father's hands, the way the fingers naturally curved when the hand relaxed. When I began to cut his hair, he trained his eyes on my hands. "You do not realize it," he said, "but you are cutting away at my life too, time leaving me like moments falling to the floor."

I was afraid of him, Lupe. Suddenly, I was afraid of a man I could easily destroy with one swerve of my razor, with one jolt of my scissors. A man who was a great lover, not a great philosopher. I didn't want to hear philosophy. I wanted to know about the desert at night, the ride of the four horsemen, the posture of the tango. But he was speaking about death, his own death. And he was implicating me. But most frightening of all, I had this disturbing feeling he was right. He was dying. I was dying. We were all dying at this moment, in this place, with only the light as witness.

Somehow I gathered my courage and told him he had something all men wished they had. And that it was not his money or his appearance. I suppose I was being rather bold because he immediately looked directly at me, causing my scissor to glance slightly off of his left ear.

He just looked at me. Didn't say one word. He just looked and looked into my face. It was then I realized he was waiting for the answer. I told him what he had was a way with women. And in a vain attempt to guide him away from his despondency, I told him about the woman I was in love with but who did not even care if I lived or died. Honestly, she did not really know I existed. Oh, she was a friend of a friend, and we talked, but I could tell she was not fascinated by me. I still cannot bring myself to speak her name. It was odd to tell this to Rudolph Valentino, a man who had probably never been scorned by a woman, a man who had probably made love to every woman he touched.

Well, we continued in silence. I trimming his hair, which was in need of a haircut, and he turned toward the mirror, staring into his own eyes, then once or twice stealing a quick yet puzzled glance at me. The silence in the room made everything else around us so loud. My scissors clipping steadily. The car horns from down on the street. And suddenly I could hear the young man and the exotic-looking woman in the next room arguing, at first with quick exchanges and long pauses. Then their voices grew more intense, more hateful, until finally I heard a crash or a fall, I really wasn't sure which. But I could hear someone crying and gasping and trying to talk, trying to defend. It was the young man's voice. I think she had hit him with something. Valentino's eyes changed. "Damn it, damn it," he started saying. "Yes, I'm lucky," he said to me, "and I'll probably be lucky in hell too."

He suddenly laughed, as if he realized something was absurd, ridiculous, and far beyond his reach, as distant as his past. By then I had begun putting talcum powder around his neck and was ready to remove the white apron which was covered with his hair. His image in the mirror was the image I had seen in the dark theatre. Valentino gave the mirror his famous profile, the delicate ears, the high forehead, the angular nose. "Señor Nieves," he said, very finally, very conclusively, "your reputation is not exaggerated." And with that, he gave me a one hundred dollar bill from a money clip he had in his pocket, and he walked ceremoniously out the door.

Something happened to me, Lupe. Something seized my senses. He had said it himself: "You are cutting away at my life too." I knew it. He knew it. We all take something from each other. I got down on my knees and began gathering with these hands his hair, hurrying like a madman, afraid someone would open the door and catch me, afraid someone would see my uncontrollable frenzy.

One month later he died. It was then... it was then I discovered the magical power of the hair. It was then when I used that power. I used it to seduce a woman I loved. The woman who didn't love me.

## Chapter Two

## SNOW AND FIRE

The snow is falling, falling, like angel's hair, like soft rice, like slips of white paper with messages of arrival. It is Lupe's first snow, the snow he will remember years from now when memory and snow will turn brilliantly white and undefinable. But the snow will still be there like the blank spaces where light falls from windows and doors. The snow will still be there reminding him of its intense cold blaze.

Lupe is on the corner of 163rd Street and Tiffany Avenue when the snow begins to fall. All afternoon he has ridden his tricycle back and forth on the sidewalk in front of his father's barber shop, past the dry cleaners, the *bodega,* the delicatessen, the bakery, the optician, the sudden alleyways, the stairwells. And he has gone around the block innumerable times, first one way then back the other way. The day has grayed into a flannel-like mist; the lights on the street and in the shops have come on brightly. As the atmosphere has predicted, the snow begins to fall, in the beginning appearing as the wings of moths wildly fluttering in the air, then changing into drifting groups of small helpless birds, and finally as a great hovering of white fogginess everywhere.

Lupe remains on his tricycle, its red color standing out, a reminder to all who pass that the world is not all gray or white. The snow flakes fall to his gloved hand, simmer with a kind of animation, then simply disappear into memory and into mitten. Lupe removes his right

glove, feels the relentless chill when he captures the
elusive pieces from the darkening sky only to watch them
evaporate in his palm and become water. Undisturbed by
passersby huddling within their dark misshapen clothing, Lupe watches the streets turn white and the people
walk through the darkness.

"¿Qué mira, muchacho?" a voice asks from somewhere out of the white, a familiar voice, Mangual's voice.
"Don't you know you could freeze like a statue, and then
your father and I have to chip you out of the ice you turn
into? Are you listening to me, Lupe Nieves?"

Lupe looks over his shoulder to discover his father's
best friend, Mangual, standing behind him. Mangual is
a big man, a giant, Lupe believes. In his black overcoat,
he is a great bear standing on its haunches, similar to the
Russian bears on *The Ed Sullivan Show*, the bears who
wear funny hats and roll barrels when their masters
command. Lupe is mesmerized by Mangual's overpow-
ering size, the way he looms in the air with white flakes
collapsing all over him as if he has pierced the sky and
brought it down. Lupe almost forgets how to speak and
waits for the bear to growl.

"My boy, I have watched you. You've sat on your
tricycle forever. Aren't you cold? What is it you see?"
Mangual turns his eyes in the direction of Lupe's vision,
down the boulevard of white, down the disappearing
sidewalk. "The snow is beautiful, heh, Lupe? It makes
you feel lost in it. Lost. And you wonder . . . you wonder
if you can ever find your way through it."

"Do you get lost in it ever?" Lupe finally reacts. "Do
you ever think you will never find your way home?"

"Maybe. Sometimes. Sometimes you want to get
lost in it, it is so beautiful," the big man says to the boy.
"No, I take that back. I did get lost once. Frightening. This

happened many years ago when I first came to Nueva York from the island. It happened during my first snowstorm. I thought I was walking in circles. Each block looked like every other block. Each block became my block as I approached. And then when I'd get there, it wasn't my block. I grew cold and afraid. I grew blind and numb. On a page of white I felt like a single word. *Solo.* Alone. No one was on the street. The strong wind was the only voice. Then I heard singing in the distance. But not too far ahead. I heard one voice then more than one. The voices of song and the sounds of tambourines came closer and closer. And then I saw them," Mangual says, and he raises his large hand in the air and points in the direction Lupe has been watching, towards the boulevard.

"Who did you see?" Lupe asks quickly and curiously, following the movement of Mangual's great hand.

"I saw the hallelujahs. A group of six or seven beating their tambourines and led by the old *bruja* who had her mission in a store on my block. One by one by one I could make out their shapes as I walked faster and faster, almost crawling over the deep piles of snow. The *bruja's* bright red scarf was really the first sign that I was home. When I walked past them, they didn't seem to even notice me, they were so involved, so fixed in their song, their revery. But the *bruja* did. I'd swear her special eye followed me as I went past them. I tried not to think about it until later when I was in my little warm room. Why were they out there shouting and singing and beating their tambourines in the snow? It was almost as if they were a lighthouse calling me to safety. I saw the *bruja* many times after that but never dared ask her. Never really dared. Whether one believes in *brujas* or not isn't what's important. What is important is that *brujas* believe in themselves, and that's their power. So if the

*bruja* wished to dance on fire, I would not ask her why.
It would not be my place to ask her why," Mangual
completes his story and shakes in a cold dance of his own,
his rubber boots stomping and crushing open holes in the
snow.

"Were you a little boy like me?" Lupe asks.

"No, I was a man by then. A young man. In fact,
shortly after that I met your father Facundo Nieves.
Funny I should meet a man named Nieves after such a
strange event. But I felt we were meant to be friends the
day he cut my hair. He gave me a good tip on a horse that
day. He gave me a lucky horse too. Your father used to be
a very lucky man in those days. A man's luck changes
though with time."

"He's not lucky any more, Mangual?"

"Well, I don't mean that. I just mean things were
different for him then. When you're young, you're freer,
you're not afraid to experience things like when you're
older. I mean, look at you, Lupe. You're free to ride that
bike, you're free to watch the boulevard fill with the snow,
and you're free to discover things. So maybe now you're
the lucky one, huh, Lupe? And your father is lucky
because he has a *muchachito* like you. You are his shiny
penny. You are even a lucky age. Seven. A lucky number.
*Mucha suerte.*"

"I will be seven soon. I'm still only six. Six is not
lucky?" Lupe keeps questioning.

"Well, in some cases it might be the sign of the
devil," Mangual mumbles impatiently under his breath,
"but no, I don't mean that, my boy. You know something,
you think too much. You know that? Maybe you'll be a
philosopher. Just what your father needs these days. You
shouldn't think so much. Especially in the middle of a
snow storm. Your thoughts get cold and fall to the ground

like frozen dogs, and the street cleaners come pick you up and say that he froze because he thought too much. Look at that sky," Mangual says as the grays grow almost black.

Lupe looks up, then ahead, and is deeply drawn into a spot of movement on the sidewalk across the street, a small figure treading slowly along and occasionally disappearing behind a car. Mangual turns his attention to the child Lupe is watching. It is a little girl a few years older than Lupe. She is bundled up in her oversized coat which almost touches the tops of her shoes. Her blue leggings are slightly seen when she takes her careful steps. She is carrying a brown grocery bag, and she switches it from hand to hand, only to finally hold it in both her hands and to her chest. But suddenly she drops it at the point where she is almost directly across the boulevard from Lupe and Mangual. A plantain and an onion roll out onto the snow, but she scoops them up clumsily, dropping them again, and as she does this, she catches Lupe's gaze. She does not acknowledge him, nor does Lupe react, but Mangual chuckles and snorts white smoke from his nose.

"Do you know her, Lupe?"

"Dolores," Lupe says simply and without emotion.

"She's very pretty. You don't like her?"

"She does not like me," the boy in the snow continues.

"But why?"

"She makes fun of my leg. She tells everyone I have a Frankenstein leg."

Mangual is obviously confused by this. He looks down at the corrective boot Lupe wears, the heavy leather shoe which is meant to straighten his clubfoot. "Why Frankenstein? You are not ugly like that beast made from dead men's parts."

"In the movie, Mangual, the ugly man has these big shoes, and he walks funny, and that's what she says I am like. And she says that this isn't my real leg, and that when I was born, I didn't have a leg, and that the doctors put this crooked leg on me and got it from a dead baby, a baby the doctors found in a garbage can," Lupe tells Mangual while still staring at Dolores, who by now is crushing the bag closed. "She says it is true. She says her mother told her it was true."

Mangual does not know what to say to the boy. Children are cruel as winter. "She has a pretty face for a liar, Lupe. Maybe you should just give her the evil eye, little one. Huh? Yes, *brujas* come in all sizes. Come on, Lupe. Let me help you with your tricycle. Let's go back to the barber shop and get a bit of *café*. Heh? Your father is probably wondering why I am late and why you are not there to help him. Old men like us get impatient, you know, when death breathes down our necks," he mumbles to himself.

Lupe dismounts and Mangual picks up the tricycle with one hand and reaches for Lupe with his other hand. Lupe puts his small hand in Mangual's bear-hand and says, "It's too bad she is so pretty. It's too bad she must die so young."

"What, my boy?"

"It's too bad Dolores must die young," Lupe repeats. Dolores is going up the front steps of the apartment building where her family has lived as long as Lupe can recall. Mangual catches a last glimpse of the little girl's blue leggings, and then she is gone into the gloomy hallway.

"You shouldn't say such things, Lupe. Death is nothing to joke about. Who knows where we go when we die. It can be worse than living. Why do you say she will die young?" Mangual is curious. The boy's words have chilled him.

Lupe does not answer, for he does not know why he says this. He too is cold, and in silence he is led by Mangual the half block up the boulevard to Facundo Nieves' barber shop. The street lights flick on. The headlights of automobiles search blindly through the snow.

During the night the snow stops falling. Lupe is in the middle of sleep. Women are screaming. He can see their necks, their open mouths; he peers down their throats, and he feels the smack of their shouts on his cheek, their sweet breath on his face. They are screaming and screaming until they become so loud that Lupe awakes. From underneath his bedroom door a sharp crack of light rises and covers the walls. The light in the hall is on. The floor he treads barefoot upon is cold like the snow. When he opens the door, he calls for his father, and the women keep screaming. All the lights are on in the apartment. The rooms are bright to his sleepy eyes. Facundo Nieves is not in the apartment, and the women continue screaming. Lupe's eyes begin to tear. He is alone. *Solo*, as Mangual says when lost in the snow. Lupe goes to the apartment door, for he hears the screaming women outside in the hallway. They are hurting his father; he is sure he will open the door to blood smeared down the long hallway which leads outside, the hallway which takes him to the snow-covered sidewalks, the sidewalks Lupe sees every day of his life when he opens the door of his father's apartment.

But when Lupe swings back the door, the hallway is bright with reds and yellows, and at the end of the hallway is a clutter of people. Lupe, barefoot and in his pajamas, limps awkwardly down the hallway. His bad leg slows him, and he grips the walls for support. The people too are in their sleep-clothes, and they are huddling in the entrance of 979 East 163rd Street, their faces brightly lit by flames, their faces composed of light and shadow. *Fuego, fuego, fuego.* The word itself lights up the street. The word shapes their mouths. The word begins to form in Lupe's throat, forms on his winter-chapped lips. *Fuego, fuego, fuego.*

No one notices Lupe as he works his way through the gathered crowd. He stands barefoot in the snow looking up at the apartment building across the street. The top floor apartments are blazing with fire, and the screaming women are the sirens of fire trucks and police cars blocking the boulevard while ladders stretch up the side of the building and into the fire which reaches and flashes and quivers like a growing thing. *Fuego.* Lupe stares up at the source of the flames, the windows exploding with smoke and with hot light. For an instant he sees Dolores, her arms waving, her body drowning in smoke. Lupe is sure she also sees him, standing erect in the snow, his crooked leg cold and numb but strong, for that moment dependable. *Fuego.* She disappears into the flames with a spark of silence.

The enflamed world grows quiet, the sirens submerged in the watery sounds of fire hoses, the voices of the onlookers lost in the waves of light sweeping across the streets. And Lupe is being lifted up, above the snow and lights, closer to the fire, to the warmth. The familiar smell of cologne rises above the burning.

"Lupe, what are you doing out here? You're practically naked. Oh, my god, and barefoot too." Facundo Nieves holds his son in his arms and tries to warm him, the cold feet first. Nieves wraps his tweed coat around Lupe.

"I woke up and you weren't there," Lupe says, his lips trembling. He presses himself hard against his father's chest. "I saw her. I saw her at the window. She was on fire."

"Who did you see?" the bespectacled barber asks.

"Dolores," Lupe says. "I saw her at the window. She was in the middle of all the smoke. She saw me. She was looking down at me. She knew what I was thinking. She knew I did it."

"Did what, Lupe? What did you do?" Nieves' voice echoes in the hallway of the apartment building as he carries Lupe, taking him away from the excited crowd and the cold night air.

*"Fuego. Fuego,"* Lupe whispers and hides his face in his hands. He is shivering. He has never felt such cold.

"You were asleep, my son, when the fire started. You didn't do that. You didn't do that," Nieves says, consoling the boy as they both enter the brightly lit apartment. "I must shut off some of these lights. I couldn't believe it when I heard there was fire. I thought we were on fire, and I just panicked and turned on everything to pack us up if I had to."

"But, Poppi, I knew about it. I knew something would happen to Dolores. I told Mangual. I saw her. She saw me," Lupe insists.

"Stop it, Lupe. Stop it, my boy. You will make yourself sick."

"But I saw her, Poppi."

"That's impossible, Lupe. Impossible. Maybe you had a premonition. Maybe a dream. No? That's happened to me. Many years ago it happened to me," the barber assures him.

"What's premonition?" Lupe asks. To warm Lupe his father serves him a *tazita* of black coffee with lots of sugar. "What is that word?"

"A premonition is when you have a feeling, a sudden feeling that something is going to happen. It is a mystery, but it happens to some of us. We just look into a person's face sometimes, and we know something will happen, something good or bad, but something lies ahead in that person's future. And we know what it is, and we may even feel horrible that we know about it. But there's little or nothing we can do to stop it because it is destiny. It will happen no matter what." Nieves looks older and more tired than he did yesterday, than the day before yesterday. "It is a gift, it is a curse, this premonition."

"But I saw her at the window staring down at me. She knew that I was there. And she hated me for being there to watch her burn up. I watched her get burned up in the fire. Poppi, she just stared down at me with her eyes of fire."

"Lupe, my boy, that's not possible. Listen to me, now. It's not possible. Someone set that fire, but it wasn't you. When the fire began, all the families on that floor must have been trapped. Some were able to jump out to the fire escapes. But her bedroom had no fire escape. She jumped from her bedroom window. Listen to me. She jumped, Lupe, to the sidewalk. She was killed from the fall. I don't know what you saw, my son, but she was already dead. She was one of several who jumped to their death before the firemen even got there. Do you understand? Listen to me. Do you understand?"

The boy begins to cry. He feels like he can cry forever. His tears are cold. His tears are hot. He cries himself to sleep. He cries for the snow. He cries for the fire. He cries for the ghosts in his dreams.

## Chapter Three

## DREAM OF THE WALL

Lupe hears his father shaking loose the morning paper in the kitchen. The smell of coffee is filling the apartment. Lupe is finally awake. He has had a dream. It keeps returning.

When it happens, he thinks he is awake. He looks around. It is still dark in his room. The windows are mute slaves to the wall. He has been dreaming about the wall. What was the dream? He tries to recall but whispers across to the bedroom wall for help. It leans back blank and gray except for a plastic crucifix.

He hears the ticking of the Big Ben. The ticking grows louder with each tick, with each passing second. The wall begins to move, one almost unnoticeable step to the sound of each tick. And he begins to think about a photograph of his father holding a bundled baby in his arms; he is standing on the corner of 75th Street. His father is dressed like a gangster. He sees a photograph of his mother, Antonia. She is smiling, curtsying, her dress held out by her dainty hands. It is a birthday picture, but it could just as well be a wedding. Antonia always looks like a bride in pictures.

To the sound of each tick, very slowly, from the crease of the corner where the two walls meet, light appears like a fine long blond hair. Lupe thinks of New York snow first falling, and it is the first winter he stands up on his own, wearing the shoes his father buys him to keep his crooked leg in place. Through the early snow he

rides to the corner on his tricycle. The bright red stream-
ers on the handlebars are blood against the white haze
beginning to change the street, the neighbors' faces. And
his own face. He stares blindly into the bright snow and
the street sign on that corner, 163rd Street and Tiffany,
the place where he meets the world.

The light grows and opens, the kind of light that
pours over the richness of its source onto the lost, onto the
secret, onto the ones who travel all night awake in their
sleep. He covers his eyes briefly with his hands, the light
is so powerful. At first he cannot see what is behind the
wall. Then he adjusts to the brilliance and sees before
him a staircase leading down into a lush meadow or
forest, he's not quite sure. The greenery is startling in its
clarity and vibrancy. In the foreground bright flowers
pose in the openness of green. In the distance there is an
ocean, the blue almost overwhelming because Lupe
hears the sounds of a shoreline which must lie some great
distance from the opening in the wall.

He rises from his bed and approaches the opening
in the wall. He knows he can never return if he steps
beyond the wall. He knows he should go, but he knows he
can't go. He knows he will never see his father if he enters
and merges with the land beyond the wall. He smells the
flowers; the ocean sings like the inside of a shell when he
holds it to his ear. In the distant sky, there are stars, stars
in the daytime. He pulls himself away. He must stay
where he is, he must lie down. The wall is closing; it
sounds like a gentle wind. The light is consuming itself,
disappearing, almost gone, when Lupe lies back down
and looks at his hand. Lines of blood crease his palm. He
is not afraid. He licks his own blood. He falls asleep again.

"Lupe," his father's voice calls, "the coffee is waiting
for you."

He opens his eyes.

*Chapter Four*

## MAGICIAN

"Is this the boy?" Barbara casually asks her father after peeking through the open door of apartment #2 one spring afternoon. "He looks colored, Dad. Is he?"

Lupe is nine years old and unfamiliar with the term "colored." Later he spends time in front of the bathroom mirror looking for the color in his pale skin and inspecting his pink tongue and gums.

"No, he is just a Puerto Rican boy, heh, Lupe? He is just a bushy-haired boy of Nueva York. *Entra*, Barbara," Nieves responds to her question, trying to pull her away from her own words. "How long has it been, my daughter?"

She ignores her father. "He seems to be walking well too. I thought you said his leg was improving very slowly."

"He has to wear a special shoe. Show her, Lupe," he says, and Lupe puts out his right foot and lifts up the pants leg to reveal the leather boot. "When he was born, the left foot was perfect in every way and pointed straight ahead. But the right foot was twisted and pointed the reverse; poor boy looked like he was confused and was walking forwards and backwards at the same time. A foot in this world, a foot in another world. He still gets pains in his leg, but the massages help. The leg will straighten out. Maybe someday he will walk without tripping. Right, Lupe?" Nieves says. He caresses the boy's head of hair.

"His hair is so thick and kinky. Maybe you need to straighten that too, Dad," Barbara continues. She reaches back out into the hall and drags in her own daughter, Ellen Jane. "This is your grandfather, Ellen Jane. Do you remember him?" The girl does not react. "You met him at your grandmother's funeral. Since you asked how long it has been, it has been a little over two years," Barbara tells her father. "A little over two years since my mother died. I must admit I was surprised you came to the funeral. But I was glad you did. Considering everything. Considering you two hadn't seen each other in ages." Once again Barbara turns to her daughter. "Well, say something to your grandfather." Ellen Jane murmurs something that is inaudible, almost the shape of language. "She's so shy," Barbara says once the silence gives her reason to explain her daughter's inability to mouth her words.

This girl is definitely colored, thinks Lupe, peachy and blond, with red lips and red cheeks. If anything, Lupe looks rather neutral and flat next to her. She is about Lupe's age, but she is taller, and as she enters, she stares down at him with hostility and aversion. Ellen Jane does not wish to be in the heart of the Bronx where the one language she knows becomes two languages, where there is no acceptable uniformity to the people as in her town.

"So I see." Nieves begins cautiously, "She is shy, and my son has curly hair, and he is a full-blooded Puerto Rican. And I, your father, am a full-blooded Puerto Rican. None of this can be helped. None of it. His mother is Puerto Rican. Your mother, may her soul be resting comfortably, was Puerto Rican. But, *mi hija,* I have never fooled myself into believing that you think of yourself as Puerto Rican. You have always run as far away as you could from this. But this boy, this boy, well, he is, beyond

anything, the image of myself when I was a boy on the
island, when I was growing up swimming in the ocean
and exploring the coves and fishing for the big fish." And
Nieves leads all into the kitchen where the light is best.
"*Pues,* how are you? How is Raymond?" Raymond is
Barbara's fair-skinned American husband, the fire chief
in the small Ohio town where the family lives.

"He is very well. We are going to adopt a little boy,
a brother for Ellen Jane." Barbara Nieves Parker has not
been able to have children after Ellen Jane's birth.
Finally, she has convinced her husband to adopt what he
refers to as "a little stranger."

"Raymond is willing then to adopt. *Bueno.* That
indeed is a miracle," Nieves responds. "I am happy for
you, Barbara." He reaches across the table and squeezes
her hand gently, an affection clearly in his eyes which
causes envy in the boy. Lupe swears Barbara flinches at
her father's touch, not with hatred or dread, but with the
kind of repulsion Lupe also senses from Ellen Jane.
Nieves asks his son to take Ellen Jane into his room and
show her his newly painted rocking horse which Nieves
has made. But the little girl does not want to leave her
mother's side and sits at the table, peering with curiosity
at this new grandfather she is trying to recall and this
little boy who has been introduced as her uncle.

Within minutes, Barbara is smoking her third
cigarette. She smokes unfiltered cigarettes, the same
brand Nieves smokes.

"*Ella es mi hermana,*" Lupe suddenly interrupts.

"Quiet, *muchacho,*" Nieves demands, a detectable
smile on his lips. Nieves looks deeply into his daughter's
eyes and asks, "Do you know what Lupe just said? Do you
not remember your native language?"

Barbara inhales slowly, deliberately, then exhales

through her teeth, almost with caution. "I remember my Spanish, Dad." No one ever calls Nieves "Dad," Lupe thinks. "I remember a lot of my Spanish. Maybe more than I want to. I just don't use it anymore. I have no real need for it anymore. And you and I, well, frankly, we see each other just every once in a while. Right, Dad?"

"But what did Lupe say?" Nieves pursues further. "What did he say?"

"Lupe said that I am his sister," Barbara responds. "Right, Lupe?" she asks the boy directly across the kitchen table. "Actually, Lupe, I am your stepsister. Do you understand that? You and I have different mothers. Your mother is Antonia. My mother was Mary."

Lupe nods. Sweat begins to line the inside of his clothes. He doesn't understand. And he doesn't understand this woman who has walked into his life from the cluttered and familiar streets.

Nieves silently gets up and begins preparing coffee. "How about *café con leche*, Barbara? I bet it's been a long time since you have had the real thing. Lupe, take Ellen Jane into the living room to watch a little television, huh, my boy. Howdy Doody must be on by now. I will call you when the coffee is ready. We can have that with some fresh coffee cake I bought only this morning. Go on," Nieves gently commands. The children are gone, and the old barber continues talking to his daughter. "You know, Barbara, I love you. Always. But I love Lupe too. Now he is all I have, all I live for really. He needs me. You do not need me. And yet if you did, I would do anything for you, anything I would be capable of doing."

Barbara gets nervous at the talk of love. She gets up and walks to the window. The shadows at this time of the afternoon are very dark across the alleys. She watches a woman leaning out of a third floor window; the woman is bringing in the sheets off of the clotheslines. Barbara remembers the clotheslines stretching from building to building. When she was a girl, she thought the lines held everything up, the buildings, the women's lives. Those clotheslines were the only connections to anywhere, to anyone. "Dad, did you love my mother? I mean did you really love her more than anything?"

"Why do you ask me this, Barbara?" Nieves states without looking away from the stove. "Why? Have you always wondered this? Have I done something to bring this question out from you?"

"Dad, it's just that before she died she told me that she always felt that you never really loved her. That there was always someone else back there in the back of your mind or your heart. That you were always distracted by the memory of this other woman. I believe Mom told me that this other woman was someone who had died and that you never really got over it. I don't want to come here and dig up painful memories, but I guess I just would like to know. I didn't have the heart to ask you at the funeral. You did seem so sad, so sincerely sad," Barbara drifts off.

"I was," the old barber confesses as he places the silverware on the table. "I really was. Your mother and I were not married long. Five, six years. I respected her. I respected her very much. She was a good woman who really deserved better. But, my god, I was merely a stupid, clumsy barber she fell in love with. After the stock market crash in 1929, I lost one barber shop, then another. I met your mother after that, and she saved me with her gentleness, her kindness. I was always glad she found someone else after me. And, yes, I did love her, loved her deeply, loved her like the sister I never had. But I became the center of her world and couldn't feel the same about her. I must admit, though, when you were

born, you became the center of everything. You were my
first child and will always be my first. And you kept us
together for awhile longer than we would have. You gave
us hope for awhile. A child can do that, can't it? Then
before the Second World War began, she was gone, you
were gone, and I was alone again," Nieves says to
Barbara, who turns away from the window to face her
aged father. "It was sad. I couldn't comprehend why I was
not permitted to love the woman I really wanted."

Silence settles between their words, between the
stirred spoons striking the inside of the coffee cups. Next
door, Mrs. Sanchez's cry from her window overlooking
the super's yard briefly interrupts this moment between
father and daughter. She calls her son home, home from
the alley where he stands and responds to her cry.

"Barbara, that woman, that woman your mother
never met, died in my arms. Right here," Nieves says
raising his arms close to his chest as if he were holding a
child to him. "Right here in my arms. How can a man
forget that? How can anyone forget someone you love
dying in your arms? Could you, Barbara? Could you?"

Barbara begins to respond, to stutter a response,
but the children suddenly laugh in the next room, laugh
loudly together at something amusing on the television.
She looks at her father and smiles. Nieves wipes his
forehead, takes off his glasses, cleans away the fogginess,
and speaks slowly. "And so after the war, my daughter,
I discovered I was much more stupid than before the war
because, like a foolish old man, I married the much too
young Antonia Ramirez. That is your father's story,
Barbara."

"I am sorry, Dad." For the first time, Barbara
reaches out and puts her arms around her father. He
feels so small, so frail; she is surprised by this.

And Nieves is surprised by her sudden emotional response. "Well, you should feel sorry for your *viejo* more often, *hija*. A hug from my oldest child is very welcome." He places the coffee cake on the table and begins cutting slices.

"I am curious about something else, Dad," Barbara tells her father as she lights another cigarette. "Your magic. Your crazy Puerto Rican voodoo."

Nieves slows his movements and looks up at his daughter, squinting his eyes slightly. "What do you mean?"

"Mom told me you did some kind of magic. She said doctors had told her she could never get pregnant. But then suddenly she was pregnant. She said it was your magic. All the time she was telling me this, I thought she was joking. I almost laughed. If it wasn't for all the tubes going in and out of her, I guess I would have laughed. She seemed so serious."

"Ah, but your mother was always a serious woman. Hardly ever laughed out loud. Hardly ever showed emotion."

"How about Antonia?" Barbara asks.

"What about her?"

"Mom said you fooled her, you did something with magic to get her to marry you." Barbara sips her cup of *café con leche*. "Wonderful. You have not lost your touch."

"Thank you." Nieves sits down and lights a cigarette. "Antonia thought I had money. How funny. She thought I had money because I owned a barber shop. She did not understand I lost all my money years ago."

"Well, Dad, you never should have married such a younger woman. I mean you were thirty years older than her." Barbara reaches for a piece of cake.

"Antonia would stand at the window and watch the

street for long afternoons. She would adjust the window
blinds, flashing them open and closed. It wasn't until
later that I realized she was signalling Louie Toro,"
Nieves admits.

Barbara puts down her fork. "You mean she was
seeing Louie Toro while still married to you?"

"Well, like you say, I never should have married
such a young woman."

"Dad, you're sixty years old," Barbara says. "I guess
you're lucky to have an ex-wife who actually lets you keep
your son with you most of the time."

Lupe is standing at the doorway. Barbara and
Nieves turn to each other, not sure how long the boy has
been listening. "Poppi, can we have some cake?" he asks.

"Of course, *muchacho*. Bring Ellen Jane in here,
and I will serve you both some cake." The two children sit
across from each other quietly eating. Lupe has black
coffee; Ellen Jane prefers milk. "He's learning to write
English very well," Nieves tells his daughter. "I caught
him writing in crayon last week on that wall." He points
to the wall opposite the kitchen table. "I asked him what
he was doing. He said he was writing a song. He said he
was writing it in English. I was glad and pleased. Antonia
won't let him speak anything but Spanish when he's in
her house."

"How is Antonia?" Barbara asks with a kind of turn
in her voice, for she really does not care. It is her
inquisitive nature which questions Nieves about his
second wife.

"As immovable as the Empire State Building.
*¿Qué mas?* She still refuses to accept the English language; that's why I am so glad Lupe is learning so much
at school," her father explains. "She and Louie Toro have
a little boy. He'll be ready for his first haircut soon. But

she is unhappy as usual. Nothing ever satisfies. Problems. Always problems."

"And does she say you used magic? Does she say you put a spell on her? Does she?" Barbara is determined to confirm or condemn her dying mother's words.

Nieves raises his shoulders and rubs his forehead. "What should I tell you? She was a very pretty young woman. I knew her father, Severo the candymaker. My father too was a candymaker in Aguadilla. Antonia wore those off-the-shoulder bright sun dresses the women on the island would wear on hot days. I bought coconut candy from Severo and decided she reminded me of my island which was strewn like candy in the Caribbean." Nieves pours Lupe another coffee. "Magician," Nieves abruptly responds.

"What?" Barbara shows interest, but Ellen Jane wants to go to the bathroom, so Barbara is briefly interrupted. She heads her daughter towards the hallway.

"Antonia called me a magician. One time even a witch doctor. But to be called a witch doctor seems so primitive." Nieves offers another piece of coffee cake to Barbara. Lupe touches his arm indicating he wants some too. "Dad, you let him drink all that black coffee?" Barbara says with astonishment. The look of disapproval on her face is enough to make Lupe feel avenged for the insecurities she evokes.

"He likes it with sugar. Lots of sugar," Nieves calmly responds. He pours the boy another *tazita*. Then without looking at his daughter, Nieves says, "I could have helped you and Raymond. If you wanted to have a child, I could have helped you with a powerful talisman."

There is some truth then to her mother's dying voice. The dead are to be believed, perhaps more than the

living. "No," Barbara firmly responds. "I must say no."
She suddenly appears to be afraid of her father, afraid
but trying to appear unafraid.

"It is just as well. You will take a little orphan into
your house. But if you ever need me, I am here."

Ellen Jane's voice rings from the bathroom. She
cannot reach the handle to flush the toilet, she says.

They drink coffee in silence. Lupe asks for one last
cup, and shortly thereafter, Barbara and her daughter
disappear out the door, down the pee-stained entrance to
the building, into a taxi cab, and into the hungry street
as mysteriously as they arrive.

My father is a magician, Lupe thinks, and he
watches his father wave them away.

## Chapter Five

## THE BARBER'S SHOP

Nieves' barber shop is a storefront, among many storefronts, on the first floors of the apartment buildings lining both sides of 163rd Street. The shop has a worn red, white, and blue barber's pole outside by the entrance. The colors once turned and swirled, but when the pole stopped working, Nieves did not repair or replace it. So its last turn of colors stays fixed in time just like its owner. There is a glass display window, and in the display area Lupe's father places large free-standing placards for advertising men's hair styles and hair products.

One placard shows a handsome, slick-haired man from the chest up, staring out to his left at the people on the sidewalk; he is surrounded by three admiring cardboard women whose eyes are trained on his haircut. The caption at the bottom reads: "Where are you without him ... your neighborhood barber." But below that, in Nieves' elegant and seriffed handwriting, is the Spanish translation: *En donde esta sin el ... tu barbero del vecindad.* At night when the store closes, Nieves shuts the accordioned, heavy metal gates across the man and the women, across the plate glass window, across the entrance and the barber shop pole, keeping out those things no one knows, keeping out those things no one cares to see.

To the right of the display window is the entrance, a hardwood door, half glass on top, with the numbers 955 in silver paint on the thick glass. Within, the shop is long but not very wide. On the left are three barber shop chairs and a mirror running the length of the wall, along with sinks and counter space cluttered with bottles of fragrant lotions. On the right are chairs, hat and coat racks, and stand-up ashtrays. A doorway at the rear of the shop leads to a back room.

This small room is lit by a single light bulb suspended from the cracked ceiling. Several boxes are stored in the room, and there is a bathroom which is used by the customers as well as Nieves' employees. A small gas stove, on which Nieves heats meals and makes *café con leche*, is by the bathroom door. Above the stove is a plywood cabinet where canned goods are kept. Mario, a barber in Nieves' shop, keeps a loaded pistol in the cabinet for protection against holdup men who threaten the businesses in the neighborhood. Mario, who is very old and almost deaf, claims he took the gun from an enemy soldier in World War I, but his customers laugh and ask if he has confused his wars, for it looks as old as a relic from San Juan Hill. Nieves tells Mario that a razor would be of better use than an ancient gun locked away in a back room. "Don't worry, boss," Mario responds in broken English. "I will kick him in *los huevos y* then I get *mi pistola.*"

Also in the back room is a high window with bars. Through this window Nieves can look across the enclosed alley and see Lupe at the living room window of Nieves' first-floor apartment. He sees the boy watching television; he sees the bright eye of the television screen and the shadow of Lupe's head before it. And when Lupe needs to talk to his father, he does not have to unbolt the front door and walk down the dangerous and usually unlit hallway leading out to the sidewalk. Instead, Lupe sits at the living room window and calls for his father. Nieves comes to the window, his white smock more visible than his face in the poor light, and talks across the short distance to his son.

"Poppi, are you busy with a lot of customers?" Lupe asks. The night is coming quickly. The smell of *bacalao* cooking is in the wind.

"Nobody right now, but it is still early, *niño*," Nieves' voice carries in the darkening air.

"Are you alone?" Lupe continues asking, seeking an invitation to join his father.

"Mario is shaving a customer who's going out dancing tonight with his wife. How are you doing?"

"I am alone, Poppi. I want to come over there with you." It is lonely for Lupe when his father works evenings. So Nieves gives the boy books to read, and he buys him paints to color with. Lupe also builds his version of a rocket ship in the living room; it is made of boxes and rope and string, and it flies when Lupe wants it to. In fact, Lupe's room is filled with all sorts of inventions he makes during the hours he stays alone in the apartment waiting for Nieves' day to end. "Are stars out tonight?" Lupe asks, looking up the seven-story buildings as far as he can without leaning out from the safety of the window.

"*Con mucho cuidado,* Lupe," Nieves warns when he sees the little boy stretch himself out of the window frame. It is another story down to the bottom, the basement level where the superintendent of the building lives. "Well, which is it? Do you want to see the stars or do you want to come to the shop?" asks Nieves, offering a choice.

"You want me to be an astronomer, don't you? How can I do this without seeing stars?"

"You'll see stars if you fall out of that window."

"Poppi, I've never seen the Big Dipper, except in my

book," Lupe quickly responds, referring to the astronomy book Nieves buys for him at the planetarium.

"The last time we talked about what you wanted to be, you told me you wanted to be a paleontologist. You said you liked the white dinosaur bones. You said they were beautiful. You said you liked old bones like me," Nieves jokes. He turns and looks over his shoulder. *"Bueno, muchacho*, it looks like I have a customer. If you come to the shop, lock the door behind you, unless you want to have no bed to sleep in tonight. And make sure the window to the fire escape is locked."

"Okay, Poppi," Lupe excitedly says. He loves the smell of the barber shop, the harsh lights in the mirror, the stories the old men tell, the way the street noises tie all these things together into a picture of a world he belongs in. The customers respect the lame boy, pleased that he likes to be around them, pleased that he tries to imitate their ways. Sometimes the men, many unable to speak English, ask Lupe to sing and dance along to the radio songs they hear but do not understand. And Lupe sings and dances, interprets those songs. After Lupe sings and awkwardly dances, accompanied by his broom, the men throw nickels and dimes at his feet and clap and laugh themselves into tears. Lupe wants the attention they give him when they slap him on the back or shake his hand just as if he is already a man.

But some of these men, Lupe's mother Antonia insists, are not good examples to follow, not men of high character. Nieves also does not want Lupe to spend all his spare time at the barber shop, although he can see the boy is learning about a world he eventually has to embrace as his own. Some of the men who frequent Nieves' barber shop are what Lupe calls "whisperers"; they talk to Nieves in hushed and private conversations in the back room or at the front door of the shop, where the traffic and the people muffle the brief discussions and confuse the exchange of money and slips of paper. These men are gamblers, Antonia warns Lupe. These men are desperate.

"Desperate like your father. You don't believe me, Lupe. I can tell by the look on your face you don't believe me. But your father, yes, your father, he was desperate. He fooled me, the old bastard. He was well preserved for his age. He used that too. And he fooled me. He was older than I thought he was. And he never told me the truth. He never told me how old he really was. He just wanted a young wife. He just wanted a wife, period. He hadn't been married for years, not since the first poor woman who married him. If you don't believe me, look on the marriage certificate. Look on your birth certificate. He took twelve years off his real age because he was desperate to marry me. I didn't have to marry Facundo Nieves. Two years. That was all I could take. I had many boyfriends before him. I was the most beautiful girl in the neighborhood," Antonia says and turns around, convincing the air. "He was smart. He was nice to me, deliberately nice to me. He gave me presents. He gave my family presents. He went fishing and caught me because he wanted a son. He never had a son, and he knew I could give him a son. I have the hips to give sons," she says with her open hands behind her palming her buttocks and thighs. "And he tricked me. He got me drunk and tricked me. Everyone said he was rich. Everyone said he had money. What a lie. Well, maybe he had money, but I never saw any of it. Even today, what do I get for you? Ha. Don't make me laugh. He gambled it away. He played his horses, his numbers. He wasted his money, if he had any to begin with. Yes, he took and took and never gave me a thing. He took my beauty. He took advantage like all men do to women. Don't you give me that stare, Lupe Nieves. Don't look at me that way. I'll slap that look off your face. I will. Stop it. Stop staring at me."

*Chapter Six*

## A BLACK LEATHER BOX

It is Wednesday, and Lupe has been dismissed early from school. Lupe leaves the playground and the stickball players, walks beyond his cousin's apartment house where three boys are trying to turn on the fire hydrant. He passes his grandmother Sofia's old tenement building. Weeping is coming from somewhere deep in the throat of the hallway. He runs as fast as his crooked leg allows until he is in front of his mother's apartment building on Hoe Avenue. Lupe wonders what customer sits in Nieves' chair at that very moment, and he disappears into the building.

Lupe opens the door to apartment #318 with the key he keeps on a silver chain around his neck. It is warm and quiet inside, and he walks through the living room and down the long hallway to the room at the end, the one he shares with his four-year-old stepbrother Pipo. Lupe lies face down on his bed; he is crying, and with no intention, he drifts into a slumber. The ceiling and the walls feel close; his body numbs with the first dream, and just as blindly, he awakes. He is on his back looking up at the ceiling, but the daylight in the small bedroom seems unchanged and still bright. In the distance he hears something, water perhaps, and a voice speaking softly to itself.

Before Lupe realizes it, he is in the long hallway walking closer to the source of the sounds. From an angle which hides his presence, he peers into the bathroom.

Before him, his mother is intently staring at herself in the bathroom mirror. He sees her reflection. She is wearing a white half-slip and a white brassiere, and she is looking at her face in the mirror, diving slowly into her eyes, studying the face she lives with, becoming acquainted with herself as if with a stranger, speaking to herself as gently as to a sister or a lover.

Antonia Toro is a woman who flickers like a dying candle when she enters a room. She is proud of her light complexion which seems even fairer against her long black hair. Her dark brown eyes always possess the squint of laughter. Her teeth, white and perfect, are also set in a smile some find contagious and others find deceptive. Beneath the lovely and dainty exterior, Antonia is an unhappy and dissatisfied woman. Lupe's grandmother Sofia claims a hurricane battered Ponce on the evening she gave birth to Antonia, her seventh child and a late and painful birth. And so Sofia says her daughter Antonia's soul will always be restless. Lupe believes this to be true because he often sees storms in his mother's eyes, great waves of feeling, clouds of torment gathering within.

"Look at yourself," Antonia says to her reflection, "look at yourself." Dispassionately, her hands pull back her long black hair and reveal her face to the mirror. Her fingers touch her forehead, run along her eyebrows, search under the eyes and around the cheeks, and follow the cheekbones down to the chin and the long neck, to the throat where her hands briefly rest like birds. "*Una mujer sola, una desconocida,*" she tells herself.

Her eyes do not leave the gaze of the eyes in the mirror. She is involved with her image, feeds on its presence. Slowly, her hands reach back and unhook her brassiere, lower the straps, and remove her brassiere to reveal her breasts in the bathroom light.

She places her hands on her breasts and holds them as she stares deeply into the eyes of the mirror. "Antonia, you are getting very old. You are getting ugly. Your house is beginning to fall in," she says while keeping her very white hands on her chest. She inspects herself from head to waist, occasionally looking back up to another spot on the mirror which has lied to her.

Soon she begins to cry, but it is a cry Lupe has never heard. It is a moan. It begins so far deep within her that even Antonia stands unaware of its steady rise from her chest, up her throat, and to her quivering mouth. Her hands cover her face. It is the most natural movement his mother could make. For the first time she looks alive, she looks cleansed and real.

Later Lupe thinks what he sees is a dream, but at dinner he looks across the table at his mother's face, and he is sure she has been crying. But her second husband Louie Toro doesn't seem to notice. Neither does Pipo, Louie and Antonia's red-haired son who admires Lupe because he is permitted to travel to the other side of the avenue, to another world.

"You saw bones? Bones?" the four-year-old boy asks.

"Yes, Pipo," Lupe confirms as he tells about the last time Nieves took him to the Museum of Natural History. "Bones of these great dinosaurs. They died millions of years ago. The bones at the museum make me feel little too. I went closer and closer until I touched the smooth bones, and I thought about how they must have looked in real life. Maybe in the jungle. The bones were white like snow and just as cold to the touch."

"I wish I could go," Pipo says and turns to his father Louie Toro. "I wish I could go, Papa."

Louie Toro, a fair-haired Puerto Rican whose family originally comes from Spain, is not the kind of man to travel far to see dinosaur bones postured in the hazy light of a museum. "Maybe, maybe," Louie Toro says and nods over his plate. White rice and black beans have his attention.

"Lupe, I talked to your father today. He's coming to cut Pipo's hair, and I told him if he wants you can go with him tonight and stay with him until Sunday," his mother inserts unexpectedly. "*Bueno*, Lupe, would you like that?"

Lupe has his *maleta* packed when Nieves arrives. Pipo is afraid of Nieves and begins his tears. Upon Antonia's request the old barber has brought his best pair of scissors to give Pipo his first real haircut. Pipo continues to cry and runs hysterically through the apartment until he is eventually held down by Louie Toro in a kitchen chair. "Do it, old man," Louie Toro says. "Bless my son with the scissors which cut Valentino's hair."

While Nieves silently cuts Pipo's hair, Antonia half cries and half laughs. Pipo's locks of long reddish-brown hair fall to the linoleum. Antonia picks up each curl and puts all of the hair in a tin box she brings down from the top shelf in the hall closet.

"And now he won't look so much like a girl," Louie Toro says. And Antonia utters through a contorted smile of perfect teeth that her little boy is becoming a little man.

This is the first time Lupe sees the black leather box Nieves carries in his black bag. While Nieves sits in the living room having *café con leche* before leaving, Lupe goes into the kitchen and unlatches and lifts the lid to reveal the finest silver tools resting on faded red satin. A pair of barber shears, sharp-pointed and barely used, a silver rat-tail comb, and a straight razor with a white pearl handle are in one compartment. The other compartment, protected by an embossed and distorted glass lid, looks dark, almost bottomless. At first Lupe is not sure about what it contains. But then he realizes the compartment contains short, black, straight hair. Definitely, these are the remnants of a man's haircut.

*Chapter Seven*

## MYTHOLOGY OF HAIR

"Hair," a word common to Teutonic languages, is the characteristic outgrowth of the epidermis forming the coat of mammals. Not considered true hairs are the hairlike projections on some lizards, insects, and bats.

There are some exceptions: The hairless whale has a few coarse hairs around the mouth. The porcupine has stiff quills. The horn of the rhinoceros is a tuft of fused hairs.

The distribution varies. Different types of hair are found on different parts of the body. Mammals have a dense coat. In man and in woman the scalp, arm, leg, eyebrow, and pubic region are examples of dense areas.

Hair is found short, crisp, and wooly among black races except Australians and aborigines of India; straight, lank, long, and coarse among the yellow races and Indians of the Americas; wavy and curly, or smooth and silky, among the Europeans; frizzy, thick, and black among certain of the Mulattos.

Wavy types of hair vary most in color. But color varies less in the lank type and scarcely at all in the wooly. There are no red-haired races.

The hairiest races are the Australians and Tasmanians. The least hairy peoples are the yellow races. The lanugo on the human fetus is what remains of the covering of humankind's furred ancestors. It is mostly shed in the womb.

Hair functions as insulation. It can also cushion

hard blows, provide camouflage, block excessive light, and trap dust and other foreign bodies.

Composed of tough fibrous proteins (keratins), each hair has a thin outside layer (cuticle), then a tubelike layer (cortex), and inside this, a spongy inner core of flexibility (medulla). Each grows within a follicle. Each emerges at the surface of the skin and is lubricated with oil from the sebaceous gland connected to the follicle.

Hair grows 1/2 to 1 inch a month. If it grows abnormally long, this condition in man and woman is hypertrichosis; in animals it is angora.

Modifications of hair's natural state includes primitives fastening bones, feathers, and other objects. Victors cut off the hair of the defeated as a sign of conquest and submission. (Caesar did this to the Gauls.) Reaching adolescence, mourning the dead, and re-nouncing of the world by monks are demonstrated by the shaving of the head.

Said to have magical powers, its removal disturbs the spirit of the head, the soul of the body. The notion is universal that a person may be bewitched by means of clippings of hair. The hair is preserved from injury and from malicious users by being deposited in some safe place—a temple, a cemetery, a secret spot where neither sun nor moon can shine upon it.

*Chapter Eight*

## THE STORY OF AUGUST

Lupe, the day after I cut Valentino's hair, I closed the shop for the rest of that day. And the shop remained closed the next day. I locked myself up in my apartment and drank a bottle of rum. Now, you know, my son, I am not a drinker. I admit to many habits—women, the horses, a good smoke. I even smoked the marijuana when I was young—but I do not turn the bottle upside down. I do not fill my head with a drunkard's delusions. I thought about what I had in my possession. This was a famous man. He was like a god to me. And I had the hair of this god, the world's greatest lover. But yet I took his strength, maybe his life. For although I may be a man of few bad habits, I have one tendency which I've never been able to overcome: I am very superstitious. I'm not a religious man, but I am a superstitious man. And surely this was an omen offered to me.

So many thoughts went through my mind. I admit to you, my boy, that I was suddenly a different person. A person divided by self contempt and desire. It's strange, but I kept thinking about Samson and Delilah. When I was a young fellow like yourself, my father told me the story of the great strength of Samson, and how when Delilah cut his hair, he lost all his power, he weakened into defeat. When I became a barber, this story became even more important. Did I do that to him? I was in pain with concern. I did not know if I was a murderer or the luckiest man in New York. Or both.

I also thought of selling the hair for a lot of money. Money. Money. I was obsessed with money then. Money was the god of New York, of America, and it became my god. I saw the bums on the street and the rich men in their big cars, and I knew what was important here. I gambled and made money, and I had my shops, so I really didn't need more money. It would not be until the Crash when things would go bad for me. I then thought about what I could get in exchange for the hair. I could go to the super and bargain for free rent in exchange for the hair. The super's wife would be hysterical at my doorstep, pleading for a part of a man she could never have. Or I could get free groceries from the *bodega*. The tailor would beg to make me a new suit. Do you see what I mean? A greed was in me. All I thought of was my good fortune. I told no one. I grew selfish with my secret.

His death was sudden, Lupe. So unexpected. Yet how else does a myth die but with a stunning blow. In mid-August he was staying at the Hotel Ambassador in New York. A beautiful place. His new movie had just come out, *Son of the Sheik*.

On a Sunday, August 15, shortly before noon, Rudolph Valentino collapsed. His valet was in the suite when it happened, and he evidently called for help, for Valentino's manager, his friends. But it wasn't until four-thirty in the afternoon that the man was taken to the hospital. I've always wondered, Lupe, what happened during those wasted hours. Who can ever know? By the time Sunday night came, the doctors had cut him open.

They had cut him open, and there I was holding his valuable hair in my hand, feeling his presence. I had dreams, Lupe, dreams of his body covered with blood, his pale arms reaching out to someone but no one was ever there.

Do you know what Valentino's first words were when he came out of the anesthetic? Do you know what his first concern was? Well, a newspaper reporter in Chicago had called him a pink powder puff, had insulted his manhood and called him a coward. A sissy. So when Valentino opened his eyes after the surgery, the first thing he wanted to know from his doctors was if he'd gone through his ordeal like a pink puff. Of course, he was asking his doctors if he'd been brave. And yes, indeed, the doctors all agreed that this man had been brave.

And Valentino was not only a brave man, he was a beautiful man, which is such a rare thing. His magic held us. His magic, like Houdini's magic, made us ache for the times to last eternally, to last until the light faded from our eyes. The magic of the Twenties began to die when Valentino died.

An odd thing to be in this world of ours, a beautiful man, a passionate man. And a foreign man from a foreign country. I understood what it meant to be foreign. Valentino came as a stranger into the American paradise of the silent movie. He was from a little town in Italy. A little town like my little town. When he died, Mussolini's Fascists in New York guarded his body and wouldn't let anyone near him. Caused a big problem. Ah, but I'll tell you about that in a moment, Lupe. There's so much to tell.

The newspapers gave reports every day on the condition of Rudolph Valentino, who never really knew how seriously ill he was. It was the story of August 1926. I remember that on Monday night, the day after they cut him open, the weather was stormy. Cyclones hit Long Island twice. Sailors on J. P. Morgan's yacht thought the cyclones were water spouts and fired their cannons directly into the cyclones thinking the shots could stop them. This is a belief among seamen. My brother, who is the sailor with one arm, also believes that this is true, I'm sure. It didn't work, of course, but it warned the people on shore that the cyclones were coming.

I watched the rain flow past my windows, and I feared this was an omen. I lit a candle for his soul and kept it burning until morning. And, Lupe, I think it did some good. During that week the news from the hospital seemed to be good. Valentino was gaining according to all the newspapers and the radio. He demanded he be released from the hospital and wanted to be allowed to return to his hotel. It was Friday. Five days had passed. His temperature was normal. He looked so much better and even managed to convince his doctors to permit him to smoke a cigarette. A telegram saying, "I need you. Live," and signed, "Unknown," was read to him. Do you know what his response was? He smiled and he said, "They must have thought I was dying." They must have thought I was dying—he just didn't know. Yet I knew, didn't I? I knew the day I cut his hair. I knew it when I searched his face in the mirror, when I shaved his thin face and had to look into his eyes. I knew it, but I didn't know I knew it then. But according to everything I read, everything I heard, he was getting better.

I felt a great relief. I felt I had helped. I put away the hair in a safe place. I tried to move on with my own life. After all, Valentino had thousands of telegrams and phone calls at the hospital. He received so many flowers he asked they be given to patients in other wards. He did not need Facundo Nieves' concern. Or so I thought.

On Saturday, August 21, Valentino took a bad turn. Now as I talk to you of this I realize on that Saturday the customers who came into the shop behaved strangely. A very old man with a monocle sat in the chair and fell asleep as I cut his hair. He began to dream and talk in his sleep. Then he began to weep, and I shook him very hard to pull him out of his sad dream. When he awoke, I asked him what did he dream, and the poor man couldn't remember. Tears still in his eyes, and he couldn't remember. And I gazed at his reflection in the mirror, and I observed the dim center of loss in his eyes. The dream had taken the glow of life out of him.

Later in the afternoon several of my regulars came in, but everyone seemed quiet and unreachable. No one wanted to talk to the barber about their girlfriends or wives, about their bill collectors, about themselves and their hopes. No. Every person who came in confided nothing to me. Gave nothing to me. They themselves were empty. Before I closed the shop many people were gathering in the lobby of the hotel and in the entrance ways, out on the sidewalk. The word was spreading like the infection which battled Valentino's body. Several people who knew I had him once as a customer came to my shop before closing to tell me that things did not look good. Valentino's temperature had risen. He had developed pleurisy, and the doctors were considering giving Valentino a blood transfusion.

I did something I never dreamed I'd ever do. I left on my barber's jacket, took my black bag, and walked out into the crowded streets. The hospital was located at West Fiftieth Street between Eighth and Ninth Avenues. I was several blocks away. So I took a taxi and arrived at a very crowded corner. People had gathered along the street in front of the hospital. It was a rather quiet kind of confusion. Many women were in tears. I edged through the commotion like a razor, slowly, carefully. At the hospital's side entrance on West Fifty-first Street, two young policemen barely worth shaving were keeping the curious from entering. And as I approached them, I never once thought about what I was doing. I couldn't help but slide through the anguished faces, the serious men, the grieving women, the bored, the thrill-seekers, past everyone. They'd all become still as a forest of trees. I felt my skin was cool despite the warm weather. My eyes were steady and looking ahead to the doorway, for it called me, it somehow appeared to open to me. And the two peach-faced policemen, as in a slow motion ballet, pushed away the others, tipped their hats simultaneously at me, opened the door for me, and without missing a step, I was drawn into the dark invitation.

They must have thought I was a doctor. It almost seemed as if they knew me or were expecting me. I'm not sure. At first I walked through the hospital corridors, up the staircases, immersed in the fragrance of the unwell. Parts of the hospital were more crowded than others, and at one point in the northeast corner of the hospital, I came upon a corridor which was silent, particularly silent, and heavy with concern. When I passed the desk at the nurses' station, two nurses looked up briefly at me, and then went right back to their conversation. I felt invisible but kept on walking until I stood before the door I knew I must enter. Chairs flanked both sides of the doorway. Someone had just put out a cigarette in an ashtray which had been casually placed on one of the chairs; smoke was rising from what was left of the cigarette butt. I stopped for a second, just a second, at the door, and then I reached up and knocked. Why I don't know. I had walked straight past the police and through the hospital like a zombie in a trance. Yet I got to the room which called me to it, and I stopped and knocked, not loudly, softly.

A nurse came to the door and opened the door wide. But when she got a good look at me in the lighting of the room, she asked me who I was because Mr. Valentino was sedated. She was never rude, a little confused, I'd say. I told her my name, and then I heard Valentino's voice say, "Come in, Señor Nieves. How kind of you to remember me."

He was pale, Lupe. He was as white as the white enameled iron bed he was dying in. He was to live less than two more days. I approached him and suddenly had nothing on my tongue, everything in my heart, and the heart has only the stupid mouth to speak for it. After some stumbling with his words and mine, Valentino asked me to give him a shave. I couldn't believe what he was saying, but he repeated this several times as he tried to fight sleep.

"Señor Nieves, I called you here for a shave," he mumbled drowsily, "and a shave it must be." And so, Lupe, a shave it was. The fastest, most frightening shave of my life. I had never shaved a dead man. But this last sign of my respect seemed to make him peaceful. Valentino reached carefully out to me. "Give me your hands," he said, and I obeyed. He took my hands and put them on his very warm face. He was delirious with fever. "Do you feel the heat of hell in me?" My hands could have been singed by his boiling blood. "Please...please...place cool towels on my face. Prepare me for my fate, Facundo Nieves." Slowly, his weak hands released my hands, and he tilted his head back on the pillow, lifted his chin slightly, and closed his dark and fevered eyes. I palmed back his hair and asked the nurse for some towels and a basin of water. I applied the moistened towels to his forehead and covered his face by wrapping the white cloth towels under his chin. He shivered and mumbled incomplete sentences, words I did not recognize. I tried to understand, but I couldn't. Then I realized he was speaking in

Italian. He kept repeating, *"Morte bella donna, morte buona donna."* That I did understand—Death is a beautiful woman, death is a kind woman. He would say this when I tilted back his head so I could shave his throat and chin. He would say it like a prayer.

I thought he was asleep. I finished wiping his face, and quietly, I packed my things in my case and was bidding the nurse goodbye when Valentino called out to me from his drugged sleep. "Señor Nieves, Señor Nieves, *cuida el pelo, cuida el pelo.*" My heart stopped. I was shocked at what he was asking of me, and the nurse must have thought I was a little crazy, for at these words I burst out crying and had to make a great effort to control myself. Señor Nieves, Señor Nieves, take care of the hair, take care of the hair, he begged of me, and I wondered if he knew what he was saying in his fever. Take care of what hair? Did he mean to tell me to continue being a barber taking care of my customers whether they were alive or dead? Or did he know I had collected his hair, that I had his magical hair, and to be careful how I used it? *Dios mío.* I wish to this very day I knew what his last words to me meant. But I was cursed to never be sure.

I nodded to Valentino, who was lying on his back and staring up to the ceiling, and I quickly said goodbye to the nurse. Out in the hallway, two policemen sat drinking coffee. They looked up at me rather indifferently as I walked away. I continued walking until I was in the crowded street among the mourners and the traffic and the police waiting for him to die.

And then on Monday the news hit the streets and spread like a wave crashing hard on top of me. Valentino was dead. It had been only a month since I cut his hair. I couldn't believe it. A bellhop from the hotel ran through all the rooms and stores, through the ballroom and dining room, shouting, "Valentino's dead! Valentino's dead!" I can still hear his voice. Women wept on the sidewalks. Men were quietly stunned. Valentino was so young that it frightened any man to think about his own mortality. Now men would point at Valentino and perhaps be grateful that they weren't him.

On that Monday I went home to my quiet apartment, and I sat and gazed at his hair. I kept it in my black leather box. I telephoned Mangual at his candy store. I had to finally tell someone. I had to talk to someone who would tell me what to do, if there was anything I could do at all. I had to do something, for I felt as if Valentino was there, alive, with me. His presence was strong. His words still haunted me: "Yes, I'm lucky, and I'll probably be lucky in hell too." Did he know he was going to die? Did he know I would be one of the last to collect these pieces of his life? Did he know he was going to hell?

Mangual came right away. Left his card game since he knew I was in trouble. I told him everything. Mangual sat like the hypnotized audience sat when I first saw *The Sheik*. When I finished my confession, I poured some black coffee for us, and Mangual lit a cigar. He smoked silently for some time. He touched the hair very gently like the hair of a child. No. The hair of a legend. And Mangual finally said after much pause that what we needed was a *bruja*, a witch, a connection with the spirit of things we knew nothing about.

We went out together into the now darkening streets and only two blocks away we stopped in front of a *bodega*. Mangual led me to the back where an old lady was counting up fortunes of small change, pennies, nickels, on her tired fingers and putting the coins in paper wrappers. No one said anything. There just seemed to be an understanding between her and Mangual, and she painfully picked up her body and led us into a room farther back. Mangual puts my case on a table and opens it to reveal the clippings of black hair. He hands her just a wisp of hair and says something like "This is the hair of a famous, important one," something rather conceited, I thought at the time. Well, my boy, she leans forward to hold it, palms it, smells it, and says, "This is the hair of one who has just died." Can you imagine, Lupe, the great thrill of fear which drove through me and Mangual. I thought he was about to faint. He began to sweat profusely and suddenly excused himself and struggled out the door into the shop.

The *bruja* eyed me very suspiciously as we both stood face to face in this small, airless room. She asked if it was alright for her to light a candle, but before I could word any thoughts, she had already lit a short thick candle which had been in the center of the table. I didn't stop her; she took a piece of the hair and touched the flame with it. I could see slight sparks rise as the dusty ash of the hair landed at the foot of the stub of candle.

And then she told me what she said I needed to know before I did something stupid with this gift. She said the hair belonged to a man who was fated for purgatory. This was the hair of a dead man who still lived. A man who walked the line of good and evil. A tormented one with a center fighting over whether to be selfish or giving. A trickster who could deceive with a glance or a kiss. She said, as she traced her old fingers through the bits of ash on the table, that it was the most powerful aphrodisiac she had ever encountered. "Whose hair is it?" she asked me again and again.

I fumbled with my words like a country boy, like a *jitano* from the mountains of Puerto Rico who has never even seen a car. But I couldn't share my secret with her, and this disturbed those old eyes surrounded by the sagging skin nothing would ever change to its original beauty. Beneath all the deception of age, the *bruja* still had a spark of passion quelled only by the fear she had if the hair was misused. In disappointment and some disgust, she told me the hair could serve as a talisman or charm. But in different love situations to mix the ash with cherry flower and root of bird-of-paradise in a beverage with strong alcohol. And one thing more, one very essential ingredient if the aphrodisiac were to possess the potency to encourage unrestrained passion—three drops of my own blood.

Yes, Lupe, my blood, the blood of the seducer to be given to the seduced. One drop for each lover and one drop for the seed of love. I fell silent. But, heaven forgive me, I was trembling with an unusual joy. The old *bruja* turned her back on me. That was my signal to leave. I threw some paper money on the table, I'm not sure how much, and I immediately left and entered the soft light of the *bodega*. Mangual was gone. Several people were waiting to pay for their purchases. I walked past them, and each of them stared me to the door, each of them knew I had just seen the *bruja*.

Only my legs carried me out, for my mind was unaware of everything around me. But I was aware of the leather case in my breast pocket, and now I was aware of what I possessed. I was also aware that it was Monday, August 23, 1926, 7:00 p.m., and that Valentino had died shortly after noon. I drifted deep in thought until I realized I was a mere two blocks away from the hospital where he had died. The warm night air was carrying the wailing of women. The moist night air was thick with the scent of women.

*Chapter Nine*

## ON THE FIRE ESCAPE

Hot days and the fire escapes are filled with the colors of the tenants, their clothes, their bare skin. Some soak their feet in shallow pans of water. Some are sprawled on their backs and stare up at the grating, at the pieces of sky around them. The drifting odors of food carry across the streets and alleys. A trio of bongo players entertains from a fire escape on the top floor across Fox Street. A breeze lifts the bright sheets on the many clotheslines. Like tightropes, the lines lead to open windows where women lean out and wilt and call out to their children below or to their neighbors around them.

"*Oye, muchacha*, you don't mean it?"

"Yes, yes, is that *loco* or what?"

"But I never thought he was like that, woman."

"Well, now you know, and you'll be more careful."

"Oh, god, yes."

"Yes. You just never know who is going to turn the knife."

"My god . . ."

"You can't even trust your own hands. One hand cuts the other. So what do you think you can get from another person but killed."

" . . . god."

Hot nights and Lupe crawls out the window and sits Indian-style on the floor of the fire escape. He camps in the half light coming from inside the apartment. Nieves does not climb out but sits in a chair on the other side of the window. And the boy and the old man talk.

They talk about the heat, the reasons for the sun burning. They talk about thirst and the stillness of the air on a hot New York night. Even the few stars they see are smoldering in silence as Lupe and his old father talk like friends into the evening.

"Did you know, Lupe, that just like people there are white stars and yellow stars and dark stars and bright stars and red stars and even blue stars. So you should never let anyone make you lose your pride because you're different. Everyone in their difference is the same. It seems so simple."

"Everyone in their same is different," Lupe plays with the words.

It grows late. Most of the windows are dark.

The super's dogs begin to bark at the invisible, begin to bark up to the fire escapes, up to the black sky full of undiscovered stars surrounded by their unnamed planets.

*Chapter Ten*

## SANGRE

There is a miracle about a razor and skin, Nieves tells Lupe. The razor sets out to clear the skin, to clear away the whiskers the skin mothers and fathers. Like a great wing, the straight edge shadows its coming. But sometimes it seems to shift on its own and throws the barber's hand into the horrible territory, the landscape of skin divided by blood, blood that appears at first as a boundary line, then spreads and overflows onto the banks of flesh. It may happen at the chin, the proud promontory of the face. Or it may happen at the throat, the fertile valley of voice. Sometimes it may happen on the cheek where it snickers red like the unplanned smile. And it may happen in rivulets or in the shapes of puddles or in the great rolling gushes of rivers, rivers of blood. But Lupe's father has the skill of a violinist, and he holds the razor like a bow making almost perfect music. Rare is the nick on a customer's face, and when it happens, it is the tremor of a sleeping face that brings red to the surface, it is the twitch of a nervous face that tensely jitters.

For Lupe, the rivers of blood remain submerged, their redness a mystery reserved for nightmares. He places his open hand on the glass window in the kitchen where the sunlight is strongest. The slight veins in his hand appear like vague worms. His fingertips glow. His hand vibrates with its own life. He thinks he can hear the pounding of blood in his translucent hand. It is the plaintive song of blood, rushing within its own captivity, always listening to only its own voice. It sings in pain, in restraint; it always harbors the hope of release until it is free to flow beyond the body. It bulges in Lupe's bad leg after a long day of vigor and movement. It pounds at the temples of headaches for revenge on the brain. It travels the heart, challenging stasis. It bursts through any exterior break and weakens its vessel, its great galleon.

And it groans. Lupe listens to it groan for five minutes or more in the warm morning sun hitting the kitchen window as he studies the shape of blood in his hand. With the beautiful light striking his face, he turns his head away. It is not his blood crying, but the cry is from afar. *Ayudame. Ayudame. Mi sangre no se para. Pierdo mi sangre. Ayudame. Ayudame. Alguien ayudame.* The voice is a cry for help. Someone is shouting that she is losing her blood, losing her blood. Lupe's whole body begins to feel the call, and he goes to the door. Someone is out in the hallway and crying for help. Lupe freezes with the dread of the doing and the undoing. Nieves does not want his boy opening the door for strangers. But this is not a strange voice; this voice calls Lupe's blood.

He reaches for the locks on the front door and unlocks each one until he is able to remove the long steel bar that presses against the door. When he opens the door, he stares down the dark tunnel which ends with the light of day ahead and the morning sidewalks. From the right, where the staircase begins its climb to the other floors in the building and where night-people sometimes gather, he hears a sinking cry. He opens the door and sets the steel bar against it so that the door will not slam shut behind him. The cry rises briefly then drops. Lupe carefully takes slow steps beyond the doorway. The sound of his boot drags and echoes.

There is no light bulb in the hallway, but the light

from the street illuminates the figure of an old lady, a slight scrap of a woman, sitting at the bottom of the stairs. In the dimness she appears to be dirtied and weary. Yet as Lupe's eyes become accustomed to the shape at the stairs, he realizes he has seen her before. She lives somewhere above, alone and childless. She speaks to no one. She comes down to the city when her needs bring her. She stares at Lupe with no surprise. But Lupe almost falls in his steps as he approaches. The old woman is sitting in a circle of her own blood, her leg slashed by a large glass milk bottle she has dropped at the start of her climb to the top of her private place.

"At last, boy, someone," she indifferently whispers. She lifts her bloodied skirt higher and reveals the gash in her thigh. The cut is big enough for a boy's head to peer into.

Lupe gasps. He smells milk and blood, and the two colors snaking around the woman have a magnificence Lupe has never imagined. "What . . . what . . ." he tries to speak.

"This is my blood," she says. "and this is my milk, and who would believe I would have both surround me, drink of me." She pats the floor, drenching her hand in blood and milk, and raises her hand to her lips. "Come, boy, do you want to taste the last of the Puentes. I am the last one, the last one," she declares in her weakness, "and I don't even know the pain anymore."

Lupe feels tears coming. "I am afraid. Aren't you afraid?"

"Afraid of what? Dying quietly and letting people walk over you? Come here, boy. Come here," she tells Lupe. "Let me show you what you're afraid of."

Lupe comes closer. "I'm afraid . . . the blood." She looks like she will float away in blood, in milk. He steps even closer, close enough for the old woman to grab his hand. "No."

"Watch the glass, boy. Listen to me. Touch this blood. It is thick as if sugar has melted in it. Touch this milk. It feels more like water. Doesn't it?"

"Yes," Lupe's startled voice answers. He does not know where his words are coming from. "Please . . . I will get someone . . . to help."

"Do that, boy. But first, taste my blood," she commands. Her hand is cold, and her grip is determined but spent. She smears his hand in her wound and tries to raise his hand to his mouth only to rub the blood on his shirt as Lupe struggles away. "You deny a dying old lady her last wish. You are a mean boy." She will not let go of his wrist.

"No, I am not. You will die. Let me go get someone to help you," Lupe says. She is still holding him.

"Please. You are my savior. Please," she whispers low and stares at Lupe with the eyes of a memory that may never end. "I share with no one else."

Slowly, her grip loosens. Lupe's hand is free to rise away. He touches his lips gently and leaves the blood there. Then he licks his bottom lip and tastes how sweet the blood is while he and the old woman stare at each other. "My father is Nieves the barber."

"I know, boy," she responds and leans back against the step, almost succumbing. "Go, boy, get help. They will replace my blood. They will bring me my milk. Go, go, go," her voice steadily follows Lupe as he limps down the hall.

Nieves leaves a customer half-shaved in the chair to see with his own eyes what his son excitedly describes. An ambulance arrives as Nieves is wrapping a sheet around the old woman's leg. Two men in white pick her up on a stretcher. She asks them if she will die. They do not respond. She turns toward Lupe and Nieves and says nothing. But she raises her hand to the boy and tries to give him a bloodstained ten dollar bill. Lupe sees on Nieves' face that he should not accept the bill, and he smiles at her as she is carried away. He has blood on his face. The bill flutters in her white hand like a blood-spattered flag carried into the sunlight.

## Chapter Eleven

## MEETING THE ONE-ARMED SAILOR

Nieves tacks the colorful map on the wall in Lupe's bedroom. This is a wall where the early morning sun strikes with its vibrancy. The boy studies the map as he stands near the window which opens to back yards of clustered apartment buildings, to the alleyway driving past the cemented backyards, and to the fire escape Lupe rides on some hot nights like a boat above the lit windows to the stars.

"I want to show you the places you come from," Nieves tells Lupe. You are from where the paper is blue. Blue for water. The life's blood of the Caribbean. Look at these islands. They are the beautiful diamonds lost by some forgotten princess. They are the gems and the stones pirates have desired throughout history and to this very day. If only these islands had but sun and sea and storm to worry about, then they could only be referred to as the most blessed in the stream of heaven. Your beginnings are from this little jewel." Nieves points to Puerto Rico. "And I was born on this part of the island. Here is a little town called Aguadilla. Well, it was a little town when I roamed barefoot. Today my town has probably grown, grown and become more complicated. Or so my brother tells me in his letters. He tells me how he dangles his nets in crowded waters. The many ships bring their inglorious goods to the shores. My mother's thatched house is gone. My one-room school is gone. The church came down in a storm. The courthouse burned to the earth one night and so did all the records proving we were ever born, we were ever married, we ever existed at all. Our memories have become documents. We begin again from nothing—*nada*. You, my son, are my something. You are my new beginning. You are my something. My something—*mi algo*," Nieves concludes with his fine-haired arms across Lupe's shoulders. "Now let me take one last look at you. It is almost time."

Lupe faces his father eye to eye and smiles. He is wearing the white shirt his father gives him, a white shirt which belongs to Nieves. "I ironed it. It doesn't look wrinkled, does it? I was very careful, Poppi. The iron wasn't too hot or too cold. I did not want to burn it like I did to the other shirt."

Nieves straightens Lupe's collar. "You are ready. You look fine. Very fine. The last time you saw your uncle Pedro you were so small you could have danced inside this shirt."

Nieves has not seen his brother Pedro in ten years, and he cannot understand how time passes almost unnoticeably, falls away like locks of hair to the tile floor in his barber shop. When Pedro stands before Nieves and Lupe that Sunday afternoon, for Facundo Nieves time becomes very tangible in the lines on the fisherman's face, in the slouched man who once stood erect at the helm of his boat.

Lupe sits at the kitchen table with the two brothers telling what they have learned over the years they have not seen each other. Lupe cannot resist staring at the stump of an arm his uncle Pedro has. It is cleanly cut from above the elbow and pokes out slightly from inside the shirt sleeve. Pedro's skin is very dark and parched by the sun that has led him, and his hair amounts to very kinky hair along the sides and back. He is bald on top, and two or three gashes are evident. Unlike the smooth-skinned and always immaculate Nieves, Pedro looks like a man whose work has tested him and whose work has won. He is a warrior who displays his scars and his losses, for he is helpless to hide them, unlike his older brother Facundo who lathers and powders and trims and perfumes and manicures and dresses his body, the world's body. And, yet, there is a resemblance between them, the kind of resemblance that can be seen in distorted caricatures. While one brother discloses the marks that never quite heal, the other brother carries the concealed imprint.

"Your grandmother, my mother and your father's mother, her name was Inocencia Nieves. She was a seamstress. Do you know I still have a shirt she made me when I was your age? No one in our town sewed like that old woman of ours. She would sometimes work day and night if a customer needed a wedding gown or a marriage suit or even a burial suit. Her fingers never failed her. Right to the very day she died, she was sewing. And she was close to blind too. It must come from her, because our whole family had good hands. Good strong hands that made things and saved things and beautified things. Your father is the same. I mean, boy, look at your father's hands," Pedro boasts. Facundo Nieves calmly pours his brother and his son coffee. "Remember, Facundo, when you carved out of wood? I bet your father never told you about that, Lupe."

"You carved wood, Poppi?" Lupe asks.

"Well, certainly, Lupe, you don't think I made you a rocking horse without knowing what I was doing, huh?" Nieves responds to his son.

"Oh, God bless him, my nephew, your father was an artist," Pedro continues. "He had the touch. He made a large wooden crucifix for our father's grave. It was so damn beautiful. So damn beautiful." Pedro shakes his head. "And then some son of a bitch steals it."

"Pedro, that is so long ago, I have forgotten that. How long ago, how long ago," Nieves mutters. "That crucifix was a real work of love. We never found it."

"Our father died so young, and our mother lived to be almost a hundred," Pedro responds, the ring of irony in his voice. "And look at us now, Facundito," the fisherman continues. "We are both old men with a trail of mischief following us like an old ragged net catching nothing. Catching a few frail fish. I remember, Lupe, your father when he was a little younger than you are now. Maybe a little shorter, heavier. He was so serious. All he loved were his books. He read every book he could borrow."

"Ah, but, Pedro, I have an added memory. One I know you could not have forgotten. The day our very practical mother told us we had to leave," Nieves states flatly and shakes his head.

"You had to leave? Leave where, Poppi?" Lupe asks.

"Leave her little house," Pedro answers. "Our father was still alive at the time. I can see that day so clearly. It was raining, and everyone was in the house. We had finished eating our evening meal, *arroz con platanos*. Our father had been very silent, almost invisible. And then, as she sat over her sewing, she said it. She said it was time the oldest made their way. You see, other children had poured forth from her like an ocean. There were twelve of us in that thatched house. The house seemed to get smaller and smaller. I was almost sixteen and in love, so I left to get married and live with my wife's family. But poor Facundito."

"Yes, how true those words are. I can look back now with almost no feeling," Nieves reflects.

"What happened, Poppi?" Lupe asks of the old

barber as cigarette smoke begins to circle their heads.

"Well, Lupe, understand my mother was a beaten woman. The children, the hard life, the lack of romance for a woman who looked older than her years. One day I came home from working in the sugar fields to find all my things out in the dirt road. My books, my poor books drowning in the puddles from that day's rains. I knew she was only trying to complete the task she had to do to force me to be on my own. I knew there was no sense in staying. She was only being a practical woman. She could break a person's heart like a jug broken at a well. But I never hated her for it. I simply picked up my things, dried my books in next morning's sun . . . ."

"But, Poppi, where did you sleep?" Lupe blurts out. He cannot understand how anyone could exile Facundo Nieves.

"That first night I slept in the cemetery. Yes, believe it or not, I slept near the tombstone of a pirate. At least, that's what everyone said about Gaspar. He was the last pirate of Aguadilla. In fact, I opened my books on his grave and let their pages dry upon the honored place where he rested," Nieves answers his son.

"Weren't you afraid, Poppi?"

"Maybe I was a little afraid. Just a touch of fear. But I was determined never to return to my mother's house. I would have held my breath and slept at the bottom of the sea that first night if I had to. That night I decided I had to become a man or join the dead. Either alternative seemed fair to me that night. Anyway, I grew up with that cemetery. I'd seen my childhood friends die of smallpox and get buried in its rich earth. My mother's mother was buried there. We even had a little sister buried there. Consuelo. She died just a baby. Our mother was so sad over her death, we thought she would never recover. I felt comfortable with the sadness of that cemetery," Nieves reveals.

"We even played in that cemetery, Lupe," Pedro reveals. "And I must tell you that your father loved to scare the hell out of his friends there too. You see, boy, that cemetery was a shortcut some of the townspeople would take. I remember one night your father sat and waited for hours just to howl like a goblin and scare one of his school chums. The poor fellow ran home with wet pants. He pee-peed in his shorts," Pedro shouts. His eyes begin to tear with laughter, and he pounds the table with his fist while his stump moves vigorously as if the unseen arm is still there enjoying the feel of the touchable world.

Nieves laughs too. At first it is a laugh slow to come. Then the smile spreads over his face, and he laughs. He laughs loud and hardy. He laughs harder than Lupe has ever seen him laugh. He laughs loud enough for all the people in the cemetery to hear. He laughs a good laugh. And Lupe laughs with them. The kitchen resounds with the sound of men laughing.

"But, Poppi, what did you do after that first night? Did you keep sleeping at the cemetery?" Lupe picks up where the story has been left.

"Oh, no, Lupe," Pedro chimes in. "No, that's how your father came to this big city."

"Well, yes and no," Nieves says. "For many days the good brothers of the church let me sleep in their tool shed. That is where I had a strange dream. It was a dream about entering a golden place, a whole world of gold and light. And as I walked, in my dream, through this light, I could see tall buildings and windows glittering in the sun. The next morning I knew I had to leave. Pedro arranged for me to board a banana boat as a deckhand, and this boat brought me to the great piers of Nueva

York."

"What about your mother?" Lupe continues his investigation. "Didn't she care that you were leaving? Didn't she try to stop you?"

"No, my son. She never even came to see me off the day the boat pushed away from her shore," Nieves concludes. "But I suppose I never really expected her to do that. She did her best. And things worked out for me, Lupe, so you shouldn't feel sorry for me."

"Poppi," Lupe hesitatingly says, "I just don't understand how a mother cannot care for her son. I cannot understand how she can throw you away like you never existed."

The two old brothers look at each other in silence. "You should know, Lupe, that I would never do this to you. And, of course, even though your mother and I do not agree on much, I can tell you that she would never do that to you. In fact, if anything, she would try to hang on to you until you are ready to leave to find your own life. The way I found my own life. The best thing my mother did for me was letting me go. I came here, and I joined the army before the war."

"Yes, Lupe, did you know your father was a soldier? Did you know that?" Pedro adds. "World War I. World War I. *La primer guerra del mundo.*"

"Well, I wasn't much of a soldier," Nieves tells both Lupe and Pedro. "I joined late and never even left for battle. But it was in the army that I became a barber. I served as an apprentice to the camp barber. You know, I did the kinds of things you do for me in the shop. I cleaned up, I swept the shop. And slowly I learned my trade. I started by putting those hot towels on the soldiers' faces. Ah, those delicious hot towels that used to put the generals to sleep and make them snore like

trains. Then because I did these things so well, I gradu-
ated to massaging their scalps. That made my fingers
strong. And before I knew it, I was holding the scissors in
my hand. The straight razor I learned fast, for this is the
skill of a true barber—to use that razor delicately, to be
able to send it on a mission to find just one whisker and
return safely to its place."

"What a lucky man you were. And look at me, Lupe.
I am the one who did not sleep in the cemetery, and I
ended up married to a bitch. A bitch, I tell you. My only
joy was looking at the open mouths of fishes and watching the beach on fire at dusk when all the fishing boats
come in. The only time I have been happy is when I am
on my boat or on the beach with a great fire going and
cooking the fish and drinking the rum," Pedro inserts
almost like a conclusion to the two brothers' lives. "That's
one thing. I am a good cook."

"Yes, you are my brother, a very good cook. You
made the best *ropa vieja* I have had in this city the last
time you visited," Nieves agrees.

"And I vowed I would do the same this time," Pedro
states. "What do you think are in these bags I brought,
Lupe?"

"Well, *Tío* Pedro, I thought maybe you brought us
gifts," Lupe responds as his eyes scan the brown bags set
on the floor near the stove.

"Well, Lupe, in a way I did, in a way I did," Pedro
nods in response. "We are going to make pasteles."

"It's been a long time since I have had those. A
wonderful idea, Pedro," Nieves tells his brother.

"My mother makes pasteles," Lupe informs the old
sailor. "But she hasn't made them in a long time. It's hard
work, isn't it, *Tío*?"

"Maybe, maybe. Ah, no, no, no. But it's not enough.

You must learn to make pasteles. Ah, no, no," Pedro keeps saying as Nieves and Lupe help him lift the bags to the kitchen table. "If I have learned one thing on the great and lonely ocean, it is that a man must learn to take care of himself. A woman is good. But when there is no woman, what do you do? Starve? Of course not. Of course not. No, what is a man on the ocean or on the land or in the air, for that matter? What a man must do is learn to sustain himself, to cook and feed on his food. You never know when one day all the women in the world disappear and get disgusted with us men because we always want to be fed. We must learn to feed them too. So today, Lupe, today is the day I teach you to make the national Puerto Rican dish, the pastele." One by one Pedro begins to reveal the contents of the brown bags.

The men work hard, as hard as women work. They take pounds of green bananas and grind them by hand until they are ground down to a great hill of mushy paste. They add salt to this mixture and a can of evaporated milk for sweetness, as Pedro says. In a large skillet they heat *aciete*; when the hot oil turns color, they add some of this oil to the ground banana mix. The hot oil makes the mix creamy and smooth and yellowish. In another skillet Pedro begins cooking cut up pork, onion, garlic, red pepper, capers, and green olives. A little bit of tomato sauce is added. The kitchen begins to smell good. Pedro begins to sing and turn the pork. He sings his fishermen songs. He sings loudly, as if he were standing on the deck of his ship.

Then the men sit at the kitchen table to prepare the pasteles, the pork and banana dumplings they will delight in later that evening. First each cook spreads a piece of pastele paper before him. On it he smears some of the colored oil from the first pan. He places a serving

spoon of the ground banana mixture on the paper. In the
center of this, he adds the pork mixture, not as large an
offering as the bananas but sizeable just the same. And
then the pastele paper is folded in such a mysterious way
that it takes Lupe many tries to complete his first
wrapped pastele. In awe he watches the two brothers
silently fold and turn and fold and turn, then wrap the
squarish shape with white string that will keep the
pastele from falling open.

As each pastele is completed, a great white heap
rises like a thick pillar on the kitchen table. It rises so
high that another pillar must be begun, then another,
until a wall of pasteles overwhelms everything in the
kitchen, overwhelms the refrigerator and the stove, the
exhausted men themselves. Finally, as the darkness
comes, Pedro begins boiling water in a large kettle, a
kettle Lupe had forgotten existed in his father's kitchen.
Most of the pasteles are placed neatly in stacks in the
refrigerator. But about fifteen or twenty of the wrapped
pasteles are tossed in the kettle to cook for a couple of
hours. These pasteles will be tonight's feast, tonight's gift
from Pedro, tonight's gift to themselves.

Nieves brings out a bottle of rum and pours three
small portions in three plain glasses. They touch glasses.
"*Salud*," the three simultaneously state. The drink is
warm on Lupe's lips. He is not sure if he likes it. Then he
feels the warmth in his chest, in his heart, in his head.
Lupe forgets himself, and he asks his uncle how he lost
his arm. The pasteles make the wet sound of rising with
the boiling water. "I lost it not too long after I married. In
an accident at a sugar plantation where I worked for a
while. Then I turned to the sea to become a *pescadore*. I
no longer felt the land was my place. Piece by piece the
land would eat me if I didn't go out to sea," Pedro says
while his one good hand pretends to bite at Lupe like a
lone sea monster gliding across the kitchen table.

*Chapter Twelve*

## SOFIA

Lupe's grandmother Sofia looks like an old gypsy woman. She wears long, colorful, flared dresses. A silver crucifix hangs from a thick silver chain around her neck. Her dishevelled gray hair is covered by a scarf, and on Wednesday nights when she attends the Hallelujah Church, a store-front down the street, she wears a white scarf and carries the tambourine she brought with her from the island many years before. And she practices magic.

Lupe climbs the long road of stairs to Sofia's apartment on the top floor. He stops at the fourth floor to catch his breath before he makes the last push up, up to where his grandmother lives in her different world. On Sofia's door are the crookedly placed numbers announcing #646. Pasted on the door are a decal of the island of Puerto Rico, its shape floating above the numbers, and a small poster, cut out from a calendar, of a black saint. Below the saint's image the tops of the letters of February can be still seen. Lupe gives his secret knock.

"*Muchacho*, what are you doing here?" Sofia's voice blares out in Spanish. She opens the door and is looking for Mishu, her black cat. "Have you seen Mishu? Oh, well, never mind," she continues without hesitation, as she ushers Lupe in. "Your mother just called and asked if you were here. Do you know something? She didn't believe me when I said you weren't here. I think she thinks I want to steal you away. And maybe I should, the way she

ignores a smart boy like you. Put those books down and
I'll get you some Kool-Aid."

Sofia's apartment is a festive yet odd place. The
hallway is lined with family photographs of the dead.
There is a yellowed photograph of Severo, the candy
maker, Lupe's grandfather, which was taken before
Lupe was born. The picture is in a round frame. Severo
stares seriously at the world as he stands next to his
candy wagon. He has his straw hat pressed against his
chest, and he looks sunburned and tired. On the side of
the wagon it reads, "*Severo's Dulce de la Isla, cinco y diez
centavos.*"

Next to Severo's picture are pictures of their dead
children, for three of Sofia and Severo's twelve children
have died. All three photographs are in the squarish
frames which can be bought at Woolworth's or Kresge's.

One frame holds the photograph of a soldier, a son
who was killed in World War II. The second frame holds
the badly damaged photograph of a little girl around the
age of ten years old. She is staring out but covering her
eyes with her left hand; there is a strong sun blinding her.
Her right hand is being held by a very young Sofia, who
looks basically the same as the old Sofia except for her
young skin and dark hair. And this young Sofia is not
wearing the thick bifocals the old Sofia in the kitchen is
wearing. There are several blotches on this old photograph, as if it has been accidentally used as a coaster.
This photograph is of Estrella, Sofia's first child. The
little girl drowned shortly after the photograph was
taken. It is often said by the family that Sofia commu-
nicates spiritually with Estrella. The last frame holds
Uncle Armando's photograph. Lupe was three years old
when Uncle Armando died, but Lupe remembers Antonia
was so distraught over his death that she tried to jump

out of a second story window at the funeral home.
Fortunately, his father Nieves the barber was there to
drag her from the frame. Uncle Armando died of a heart
attack while in the arms of another man. The family
prayed for Armando's soul. Others pitied his wife. Sofia
forgave him.

Once past the pictures of the dead in the hallway,
Lupe steps into Sofia's large and airy kitchen, the brightest
of all the rooms in the apartment. *El Gallo*, Sofia's
rooster, is chained to a leg of her old stove. He is a large
cock with black, brown, and white feathers, and he crows
loudly with the rising and setting of the sun. The neighbors
never complain. Another cry in the city air makes little
difference.

The Kool-Aid is very sweet and cold, and Lupe sits
sipping his drink and watching *El Gallo* drop two little
turds on the floor and proceed to smash them with his
large feet, as he paces back and forth. Sofia immediately
grabs him and wipes his feet and the floor. "You bad bird,"
she mutters. "You are a bad little boy."

One wall of Sofia's kitchen is covered with shelves.
Large containers for dry beans and rice occupy many of
the shelves. But the top shelves have jars of various sizes,
each jar labelled and marked by Sofia's script. Every jar
houses something different. Some jars contain spices for
cooking. Other jars contain medicinal herbs: *el ojo de
Dios, fuego rojo, mala pierna, llerba buena*. A few jars,
most of them small, have unexpected items: feathers,
nail clippings, eyelashes, teeth, and hair.

Lupe once thought his eccentric grandmother was
a scientist like the scientists in the movies on television.
But his grandmother isn't a scientist. She is a *bruja*. Or
so Lupe is told by his cousins. Sofia takes his small palm
and begins to read his fortune. "Oh, my boy, my boy, what

a sad life it is for some of us. No one deserves such a sad
life. It breaks my heart not to be able to help you."

"What do you see, Sofia?" he asks.

"Death, my boy," she answers, "but I see death
everywhere. Everywhere."

The kettle on the stove begins to whistle, and Lupe
hears Sofia on the phone in the living room. She is
arguing with Lupe's mother. Lupe can tell. Sofia's voice
is so loud it flusters *El Gallo.*

"Antonia, I'll make sure he gets to school in the
morning. He won't be late," Sofia responds. "*Muchacha,*
you worry too much. Listen, you didn't get that from me.
Worry, worry. Your son will be alright. We're going to eat
soon. *Cuidate. Sí. Adiós,*" and then Sofia hangs up. Lupe
knows he will stay with Sofia tonight.

After Sofia gets off the phone, Lupe helps Sofia with
preparing the evening meal. Sofia and Lupe wash the
black beans and cut up peppers, onions, tomatoes, garlic,
and herbs to cook with the beans. While Sofia begins
cooking the vegetables and herbs in a large sauce pan,
Lupe slices open the plantains and removes the peels.
Along with the beans and fried plantains, Sofia also
prepares rice, a large omelette, and a salad of lettuce and
blanched eggplant covered with vinegar, oil, and fresh
parsley. All this will be followed by *tazitas* of strong and
sweet black coffee.

*El Gallo* crows loudly, and the sky is almost dark.
Miriam, Sofia's youngest daughter, drags herself in just
before dinner. Miriam is only twenty years old, but she
looks older. "Hello, Lupe," Miriam says. "Ma, I got an
awful headache. I'm going to lay down in my room."
Miriam disappears into the hallway. Miriam's room is
very cluttered with boxes. The small sunken bed is in the
center of the room surrounded by the chaos of the

assorted boxes. Lupe is never sure whether she is moving in or moving out. A lamp without a shade lights the room, and the walls have peeling paint. Miriam stays with her mother because she has no other place to go.

Sofia's room is a striking contrast. She calls her room *El Cuarto de los Santos*. Sofia's soft double bed, covered by a frilly pink quilt, is in the far corner, and the walls are painted pink, except for the ceiling which is white. A small dresser with an oval mirror is on the opposite wall from the bed. And all around the room, on shelves, nailed to the walls, on the floor, are statues of various saints Sofia worships and admires. St. Francis of Assisi sits in a prominent place on her dresser. Candles are placed before each saint, and at night before Sofia goes to bed, she lights a candle for each saint and recites a short prayer. Lupe counts the saints and decides there must be twenty different prayers each night. From these nightly prayers, Sofia Ramirez seeks strength and sanity and salvation. Lupe thinks the world is fortunate that this old lady prays for it each night.

After dinner that evening, Lupe and Miriam help Sofia clear the table and wash the dishes. The leftovers are put in the refrigerator, once *El Gallo* gets his share. Lupe cannot resist asking his grandmother about her room of saints.

"*Muchacho*, they are like friends you go to for comfort. And they always provide comfort. You are your father's comfort. Yes, you believe me or don't believe me. Why does a person need comfort? Why? Let me show you why."

Sofia reaches into the cabinet and takes out some red balloons, and she begins filling one with water in the kitchen sink.

"Oh, not again, Ma," Miriam gasps.

Sofia shushes her and walks over to the kitchen window. Below, the street is active with cars and shoppers. She calls Lupe to the window.

"You are twelve years old, and by now you should know that you're going along in life, right, day to day, right, and suddenly out of the blue something happens you didn't expect. Bang! Your daughter drowns. Bang! Somebody robs you....Bang!" And she tosses the water balloon out the window and holds Lupe back from leaning out to watch the balloon take its wobbly but heavy drop to the shoppers below on the sidewalk. "And then somebody drops a water balloon on you," she says as she begins to cackle so loudly she startles *El Gallo*, who proceeds to drop a small turd. Then she stops laughing and grows very serious.

They listen to the commotion below. Many voices are shouting obscenities up to the building. But within seconds the protest dies away into the drumming of automobiles. "So you have to watch out for water balloons," Lupe says.

"And that, my grandson, is why I have my saints," she answers. "They comfort me when things are bad, when I feel bad, when the unexpected leaves me alone without help, *sin remedio*."

"I hope I help comfort you, Sofia," Lupe says, as he holds her hand tightly and brings the old woman's hand to his lips and kisses it, pressing the baby-soft loose skin of the back of her hand to his cheek for a very long moment.

Miriam watches Lupe carefully and with curiosity. The kettle begins to whistle, and Miriam removes the kettle from the burner. Sofia takes a jar off the shelf— *llerba buena*—and makes a very pungent tea for the three of them.

"Sofia, would you teach me about your magic? My father says you are a ... a *bruja*. A good *bruja*. Would you show me?" Lupe asks. Gesturing towards the jars with nervous hands, he stands by the shelves in the kitchen.

Sofia turns from her tea kettle. She walks over to Lupe and adjusts her bifocals.

"Ma," Miriam says with caution in her voice. "She hides the recipes for her potions from us, Lupe."

"Shhh," Sofia says to her youngest daughter.

"Ma, you know you won't tell him about these things, so don't play with Lupe like that. Lupe, she wouldn't tell me either about that shit," Miriam says.

"It is not shit." Sofia raises her voice slightly. "It is not shit."

"I'm sorry, Ma," Miriam recants.

"Why do you want to know about this?" she asks Lupe. She places her hand on his shoulder.

"I worry about my father," Lupe begins, eyes cast down to the cracked linoleum floor. He limps now. He limps more than I do. He gets so tired. His strength is going. Is there some magic you have to make him younger?"

"I am so sorry, Lupe," Sofia tells him with sympathy. "I have no magic to make Nieves younger. Or to make you older, although, you don't seem to need that. Lupe, I don't have the medicine to make me younger. If I did, wouldn't I use it? I'm an old lady. Wouldn't I use it if I had such a magical potion? Your father actually has more magic than I could ever have. But magic doesn't make a person young. Maybe it's something else, but it isn't our magic. Drink the tea," Sofia says, motioning Lupe and Miriam to the table.

The tea makes Lupe feel light and sleepy, and when the three of them finish, Sofia prepares the couch in the living room for Lupe.

During the night Miriam comes to his bedside in the room, unlit except for the headlights' glare. She stands by him for a long time. His eyes open, and she takes his hand and slips his hand under her nightshirt. He feels her rounded belly. It is enlarged like a small melon.

"I'm going to have a baby, Lupe," Miriam whispers, her voice beginning to sound with fear. She holds his hand there, and he senses a life brooding under his warm palm. As Miriam drops down to her knees, Lupe's fingers touch her small breasts. For a moment he envies the lips of cloth. Miriam is whimpering, "Please don't hate me for this, but I have to talk to someone. I don't know who the father is. Isn't that terrible of me, Lupe? I don't know who he is. Please don't hate me."

"I would never hate you, Miriam. You're my aunt. Does Sofia know?" Lupe's face is almost touching hers.

"Yes. But she won't help me. She told me she won't use her medicine to destroy a baby."

Lupe puts his arms out and hugs her, and Miriam rises and crawls in with him, her small body fitting along the very edge of the couch. She wraps Lupe's arm over her, his hand near her heart, and she and Lupe sleep like infants in the smooth dark mouth of the night.

*Chapter Thirteen*

## SOUTHERN BOULEVARD

On Fridays Nieves meets Lupe after school outside the playground fence. The old barber and his son walk back to their neighborhood, cutting across to Southern Boulevard towards the church where Lupe attends his religious instruction class for communion and confirmation, St. Athanasius. Lupe looks up at the front of the church; it stands unclean and grim. But inside it glimmers with hope and the words of the sisters who adhere to the doctrine of the church's saint—that the Son is of the same substance with the Father. Lupe turns his head briefly to his father, notices the slowing stride, and becomes aware for the first time that he and his father are now the same height. Nieves stares down at the cracks in the sidewalk; he too has his own thoughts.

Across the street from St. Athanasius is Mangual's place of business, a candy store with a dingy sign above the entrance reading "Manny's—since 1935." Like open gates the stained glass windows of the church can be seen from inside Manny's. Lupe often sits at the soda fountain and watches the faithful who flow in and out of the church doors. He likes to watch the faces for the changes of expression faith has the power to provide. Some who exit appear unchanged, some beyond change, the rosaries and catechisms in the white grip of believing hands, of unyielding hands.

Behind the soda fountain is a thin man. Nieves and

Lupe acknowledge him with a nod. Lupe sits at his usual place at the counter, and Nieves walks through an opening in the blue curtain which covers the doorway to the back room.

"*Ola*, Poncho," says Lupe to the man behind the counter.

Poncho looks up and smiles. He is a very ugly man. He has a large nose which has been broken in several places. His ears are oddly shaped. When he smiles, he displays teeth that are haphazardly set with great gaps marking the places for the missing. "*Ola*, Lupe," Poncho returns to the son of the barber. "Set 'em up?" This is a joke. Poncho pretends to be a bartender.

"Yeah," Lupe reacts, playing part in the joke, "set 'em up."

Poncho has the radio on, and from it comes the romantic strains of a Spanish ballad. Poncho begins softly singing with the song while he prepares Lupe his usual ice cream soda. How spontaneous and unstudied is the gentle delivery of this song about broken-hearted love. Although Poncho is so ugly, thinks the barber's son, his voice is so beautiful, so sad.

"Nieves, *cómo esta, hombre?*" Mangual almost shouts upon seeing his old friend. Mangual, like Nieves, speaks both languages well. "I can always depend on my favorite Puerto Rican to place the bets on the weekend races. Maybe someday we'll be lucky, Nieves. That special horse will wink at us almost from horse heaven, and the thousands will rain down."

"That's what I like about you, my friend. You never lose hope that the next winner is just around that last bend," Nieves tells Mangual. He settles himself on a stool and begins intently to cruise the racing news. He removes his spectacles and wipes them with the handkerchief from his breast pocket. "Well, Mangual, what the hell is good today? Or do I throw good money after bad money again?"

"Ah, negative, negative," Mangual chides Nieves. "You must think positive. You of all people who has turned the worst situations into the better." Mangual's large shadow falls across Nieves' face. "I have a good one for you. And the type of horse you are always fond of. A long shot," the big man proclaims. "A dark horse. The American Way, huh?"

"The American Way? He's a dark horse alright. I've never heard of this horse. But it's probably best."

"Well, Nieves, I got news for you. He's never heard of you either, but that won't stop his racing or winning. He's in the fifth race tomorrow at Aquaduct. And in the seventh, well, in the seventh a filly, Queen Yvonne. Forty to one. She's strong. Has good lines and good stock. Two dollars could bring a generous return. A few more horses tomorrow show promise," Mangual adds.

"They all show promise from where we sit," Nieves says to his friend, not looking up while he pulls out his worn leather wallet and begins to write down some notes in a small pad. He takes out four dollar bills and hands them to Mangual.

"We should have a cockroach piss on them to assure your fortune," Mangual jokes. Mangual sits behind a very much used card table which serves as his desk and makes a notation on a form. "How about a cigar, Nieves? They are Cuban. A difficult people, but a good cigar," Mangual adds. He hands Nieves a cigar, and the two men begin to smoke in silence, the strong aroma of the tobacco filling the airless room. But it is a good smell. It reminds them of another place in time.

Lupe is finishing his soda at the fountain when

three street punks enter. One of the *títeres* approaches the counter and brusquely asks Poncho for change, which Poncho quickly obtains from the cash register and places in the *títere's* hand. The three go out again, and Poncho hisses at them through the spaces in his teeth.

"They playing for pennies on the sidewalk. They do bad things. But you father not let you be like that," Poncho confides in his broken English. "You father use his power for you go out. Go from here and not be *títere*." Lupe finishes licking his spoon, his eyes steady on Poncho who walks to the window, stares out at the *títeres*, and walks back to the end of the counter where Lupe sits. "I *títere* one time. I was fighter. Boxer. Lightweight. *Yo gane.* You know? I win fights. But I lose bad ones. My brain, *mi cabeza, tú sabe.* My head beat. No the same now. Now I don't fight. I work. *Pero* I still alive. I no die fighting *como estupido.* I not one of those," Poncho says, pointing over his shoulder to the three punks outside.

Lupe finds Poncho likeable, almost noble. Poncho's eyes open and close quickly as he speaks to Lupe, each sentence a strain on the ex-boxer's mind, the difficulty clearly on his marked face. "You make a very delicious ice cream soda, Poncho," Lupe tells him. "I'm glad you make sodas now instead of fights."

"*Muy bien*," Poncho laughs. "Easier than fights." He collects Lupe's glass and spoon. "*Me caso esta semana.* How you say? Marry? I marry Sunday. No this Sunday. Next Sunday. *Mi mujer*, she say okay. She say she love me. She marry me. Next Sunday. *Domingo.*"

Nieves calls Lupe from behind the curtain. When Lupe goes into the back room, Nieves and Mangual are smiling at him, cigar smoke circling them.

"Lupe, this Sunday is your birthday, and Mangual wants to present you with a gift. A horse. Not a real one, but a bet on a horse, like I do. And Mangual will put the bet in for you," Lupe's father says.

"Today a horse, Lupe. Tomorrow maybe a cigar," Mangual laughs his boisterous roar.

"Come here," Nieves directs his son. "Sunday you will be old enough to be considered a man. A man must learn man-like things. Man-like good things. A cup of coffee. A cigar. A diversion with chance, with luck. A newspaper, a good horse. A good woman. These are the things a man can trust. There are few other things to share with a good friend. Very few. So today you take a chance."

Lupe stands at the card table and looks down at the horse racing sheet which is spread out before him. "What would you like me to do, Poppi?"

"Close your eyes, Lupe, and pick a horse," Nieves explains.

"Like this, *muchacho*," Mangual shows by closing his eyes and arbitrarily bringing his index finger down to a spot on the schedule of next day's races. Mangual then opens his eyes and laughs again, then puts his cigar back into his mouth and pulls and chews on it.

Lupe smiles. He closes his eyes, trusting the near darkness, and moves his right hand directly above the paper listing his choices for this first important bet. He points straight down and allows destiny to choose the horse. Mangual's mouth almost drops open to lose the cigar when he sees the name chosen. "*¡Qué milagro!*" he gasps. He takes the cigar from his mouth and snuffs it out in the ashtray. "I hope this is a sign you will always have your way in this harsh world, *muchacho*. Look here, Nieves. Look what his finger chose out of the hundreds of horses." Nieves adjusts his glasses in surprise, making sure it is what he sees. "Little Guadalupe," Mangual reads out loud. "Little Guadalupe. You have chosen your saint. Your namesake, Lupe. Oh, Jesus, and it's twenty to one. I know you won't leave this world a poor one, my young man." Mangual reaches out and shakes Lupe's hand with his very large and hairy hand.

When Nieves and Lupe leave Manny's, Poncho gives Lupe a chocolate bar. And to Lupe's surprise Poncho reaches to shake Nieves' hand but instead brings it to his lips and kisses the old barber's blue-veined hand. "*Gracias*, señor. *Gracias para tú ayudo. Me caso la semana que viene.* Marry. I marry. You bring happy to *mi vida.* You bring *amor en mi vida*," Poncho keeps repeating.

"No, no," the barber assures him, "no, you did it too. You did it too. Please do not think I did it."

Very quickly, Poncho tries to slip money into Nieves' pocket. But the old man will not take it, and they all walk out together into the sunshine the springtime has brought. Mangual and Poncho remain for awhile at the doorway waving back at Lupe who keeps turning around until they are gone from sight. Lupe and his father walk past the *títeres.* They are shooting dice against the stoop. "*¿Oye, viejo, tienes un peso?*" one *títere* asks Nieves. Lupe feels Nieves' grip tighten on his hand. Lupe glares for a moment at the punk who has spoken to his father. Together they walk past the young gamblers, taking their chances with them as they hurry to safety, to the other side of Southern Boulevard.

*Chapter Fourteen*

## ROOF JUMPER

A breezy Saturday afternoon. Autumn is in the gray air. Lupe and Nieves are eating lunch in the Kosher restaurant next door to the barber shop. Out of the corner of his eye, Lupe sees something briefly block the light from the window, and he looks up at his father's face and catches the sudden change in Nieves' eyes. A woman screams and people gather on the sidewalk around a body. Lupe runs up to the window, and between the legs of men and women who surround the lost one, Lupe determines the bloodied shape twisted on the sidewalk is a man, a young dark slim man. Nieves pulls Lupe away and tells him not to look, but Lupe cannot resist looking, he cannot turn away from the first dead man he has ever seen. The man lands face up, and although blood covers his smashed head, the dead man seems to be staring up at Lupe.

"Lupe, Lupe, come here. Get away from the window, Lupe," Nieves insists. Again, he reaches over across the table and pushes the boy back into his seat. "There is nothing we can do. Nothing. It can't be helped."

"He jumped. Why did he jump, Poppi? Why does a man jump off the roof and die? Does he want to die?" Lupe asks in disbelief.

"Lupe, everyone dies. Some men die before their time comes. Accidents, mistakes of death. Some men cannot stand to live anymore. They are in pain."

"What pain? They hurt somewhere?"

"Yes, some physical pain. Some are in mental pain. Something has driven them mad. Mad at the world, maybe. Mad at those who have hurt them. Some die for no reason. I saw a man at boot camp choke to death. During the first world war, I was a soldier, an apprentice to the camp barber. Did I ever tell you that?" Nieves asked. "Well, there was this very big man. An M.P., I think. A military policeman. He had a red face and large head and huge hands. He used to come into the camp barber shop and just tell the camp barber to shave it all off, and the barber would leave hardly any hair. He was eating lunch in the canteen one day. He finished off a whole plate of food, and he leaned back in his chair, and I remember, he said he was still hungry. Starving, he said. He went back to the line and got a double serving. He came back to his chair which was about from where you are to the cash register. And he began to gobble down the food with a strange hunger, almost a joy. I had just finished my coffee when I heard the choking. I don't think anyone really noticed because it sounded as if he was slurping up the food like a pig. But I looked at his eyes which by then were beginning to bulge out and turn red. And his red face was turning blue, almost black. His hands were clutching at his throat, and he leaped up, jerked up in position, and fell back. Several of us jumped on him, pounded his back, pounded his chest, tried to reach down his throat. Among all of us panicking, screaming, calling for a medic, he died. He just died. There must have been twenty of us there, and no one could do anything. I had food and spit on my hands and could smell it for days." Nieves sits very still. Lupe has stopped eating; he absently picks at the half eaten knish on his plate. All that can be heard is the commotion outside on the sidewalk, for the restaurant has emptied of the curious. "That told me two things, Lupe. I should never be too greedy, to eat slowly and enjoy what there is, for whatever I did not have could choke me if I actually got it. But I also realized about the persistence of death, that it finds you no matter what. I will never forget his face," Nieves fades off.

Later in the barber shop Lupe overhears the whisperers talking to Nieves about the roof jumper.

"They found a note in his pocket."

"His own blood still on it, Nieves."

"It was folded and just stuffed down into his pocket, but he meant for someone to find it."

"Nieves, he killed himself because of a girl."

"The girl he loved more than himself, the note said."

"But she didn't love him. In fact, she was marrying another man, and he couldn't stand the thought of her loving this other *hombre*."

"He could have killed her, but he didn't."

"No, my friends, if he really loved her, he wouldn't kill her. He would set her free."

"Isn't that like killing her, Nieves?"

And still, after two weeks, the dark mark of death looms like a shadow in the sidewalk, perhaps waiting for the winter snows to finally wash it away. People notice the smear on the sidewalk; they walk around it. No one steps on it. Lupe passes the stain on the way to the *bodega*. He can still see the roof jumper's eyes looking up, staring at the indifferent sky.

*Chapter Fifteen*


## MARTINEZ'S MARKET


Martinez's *bodega* is a crowded little store which always smells like *frijoles*. At the entrance are several deep bins of various types of dry beans: *garbanzos, frijoles negros y rojos, gandules, guisantes, lentejas*. The walls are covered with shelves of canned goods, many of them imported Spanish foods. Rope is strung from one side to the other like clothes lines; clipped to the lines with clothes pins are toys, magazines, and bags of spices used in Spanish cooking and herbs used for medicinal cures.

Yolanda Martinez is the owner's daughter. She has polio and is confined to a wheel chair. She is usually behind the counter, helping her mother Carmen and her father Fernando with the customers. Behind the counter there is enough room for her to move from one end to the other, backwards or forwards. But Yolanda never works alone and most nights one of her parents works with her. Yolanda is going to be sixteen very soon, and there are few choices. Tonight Yolanda is out of the wheel chair and holding herself up with her metal crutches. She is getting better at it, Lupe thinks. Her slow legs are beginning to remember the strength of the earth.

"Hello, Lupe. That's ninety-five cents," she proudly says, standing at the register instead of sitting in her wheelchair.

"You are tall, Yolanda," Lupe compliments her. "I didn't know you were so tall. You are taller than me. Does it hurt to stand?" he asks.

"It doesn't exactly hurt. It tires me. I have to do this everyday now. I'll walk someday, Lupe. I know I will," she says while putting the items in a small bag. "But see, I can hold myself up and use my two hands to do things, instead of using one hand. One day I won't even need the crutches. Are you still wearing your monster shoes?" she asks, looking down at his feet.

"Yes," he says, lifting his pants leg to reveal the heavy leather shoe which helps straighten his leg.

Lupe cannot take his eyes off Yolanda's pale legs. He wonders what they feel like to the touch. Are they soft or are they like the legs of a doll, hard and inflexible? Hesitantly, he asks if her legs are like wood or like flesh? She smiles at his question and says, "Touch my legs, Lupe. Don't be afraid. Touch my legs." He reaches out, slightly lifting the hem of her dress, and he puts his hand on her knee. It feels like a knee. He runs his hand down her ankle. This is a leg. She feels like a human being. Half her body has not been destroyed and petrified. She puts her hand on his hand. "I can't feel you, Lupe. But I'm so glad you've touched me. I have wanted you to touch me. Why are people always afraid to touch me?" she asks Lupe. And they whisper to each other so Yolanda's parents cannot hear them.

*Chapter Sixteen*

## THE FIGURE AT THE DOOR

Christmas is a week away. The sky is threatening snow. The barber chairs are occupied, and the waiting customers are either seated or standing opposite the barber chairs, facing the mirrors as well as themselves. The shop is heavy with cigarette smoke and the sweet odor of Jeris cologne. In the display window the barber's placards are accompanied by a baby Jesus in a straw basket. Nieves, whose chair is the last one to the rear, is giving Mangual a free holiday shave. Mangual is telling the latest story to pass his way.

On Mangual's last word Nieves takes a hot towel and places it over Mangual's face, wrapping it very carefully under the chin and up over the top of the head. Mangual remains quiet under the hot towel and relaxes his arms and legs slightly, enjoying the wet heat covering his skin, softening away words and memories.

Nieves adjusts Mangual's collar and powders his neck. "*Muchacho*, you have finally grown up," Mangual says to Lupe who stands at the doorway to the back room. Built like Nieves, medium height but slim, Lupe is sixteen.

Mangual is quickly up from his chair, thanking Nieves and then walking out into the dark cold. Mangual stands impatiently for a moment at the curb and then, dodging traffic, trots across 163rd Street. Lupe can barely make out Mangual's shape, illuminated by automobile lights.

Before Lupe takes his eyes away from the door framing the street, he catches in the plate glass window the face of a Mulatta. His heart falls, and the taste of fear, acid and bitter, rises to his mouth. It is Adela who has chased and tried to entice old Nieves. Adela of the streets and the curved hips. It is Adela, and she immediately spots Nieves in the back. She is coming to see him, and there is nothing anyone could do to stop her. Nothing Lupe can do. Nothing God can do.

Lupe sees her full figure appear at the door. As she stands there, two men walk out and greet her by making clicking noises with their mouths, a definite sign of admiration. She wears an emerald-green taffeta dress which holds well against her. She has satin-green pumps with a slight heel and no back strap so that as she walks, Lupe imagines, they flap to announce her entrance. And she is smiling as she removes her shawl.

Nieves is wiping his hands on a small towel as he walks toward her, towards the open front door, and away from Lupe who stands still at the doorway to the back room. Nieves talks with Adela, framed by the outline of the door, behind them the dark, broken only by the automobiles passing on the broad street. His right side and Adela's left side are facing Lupe. They remind Lupe of the silhouettes of lovers encased in a heart-shaped background on Valentine's Day cards. She is smiling up at him. Nieves is not very tall, but she is rather short, five feet or less, so Nieves seems to tower over her. She is talking rapidly but quietly, her pink lips moving like soft rubber, her eyes darting over Nieves' interested face. Nieves raises his arm above her and places it on the wooden frame of the door and leans closer to her, leans down the way a man does when he is searching shallow water for a bright coin or a shiny stone.

Lupe knows Nieves is in her already; he is not in the shop or on the block or in the Bronx. Lupe knows Nieves is no longer a sea gull with no room to fly; he is flying inside Adela, gaining altitude to her heart, to her throat, to her lips, to the small and precise ears revealed by her hair which is swept up in a French twist. And she shifts her weight to one foot and laughs out loud, a quick expulsion of joy brought on by something the barber says which she finds amusing. Her hips shift too, and she puts her long-nailed hand up in mock retreat and touches Nieves' chest, touches the white smock he wears.

Lupe feels as if he is peering through a tunnel, the periphery hazy, lost, and without detail, the center focused and hard and clear like a television screen drawing him in. His ears feel as if they are full of water; he cannot hear the distinct sounds of the voices in the shop. Mario and his customer's conversation suffocate and submerge; the two old men seated along the wall drop into the ocean Lupe knows is closing around his weakening knees; Nieves and Adela's voices gurgle and drown. Water curves all around Lupe and carries him into the black sea of the back room. He reaches up to the cabinet, for he is now tall enough to bring down the gun, which feels like a misshaped rock in his hand. Feet spread apart he lifts his arm and raises the gun at Adela. She seems to quiver at the end of the sight and sways in his view. His hand is wet, and the gun is heavy, and when he pulls the trigger, he thinks he hears the thunder of a bullet.

Nieves hears the metal sound of the spring releasing the rubber-tipped dart which propels and strikes the wall only a few inches from Adela's ear. The suction cup of the dart slaps loudly, and the dart is vibrating when Nieves turns to Lupe who is still standing in position with the toy gun in his hand. Nieves turns pale. Adela quickly hides behind him, horror on her face. Lupe has stopped her from taking his father.

"*Dios mío*, I thought it was my gun," Mario shouts.

A sense of relief melts Nieves' face, and he hurriedly walks to the back of the shop. As he rips the gun from Lupe's hand, Nieves lifts back his hand in the posture of a man who is about to slap the boy firmly across the face. But the barber stiffens, holds himself back, and very slowly reaches out to the boy with one hand, holds the boy's right hand in such a way that Nieves' well manicured fingernails are steadily sinking deeper and deeper into the back of Lupe's hand. And as Nieves does this, silence falls over the shop. No one moves. No one speaks. Lupe feels the sting of the old man's polished fingernails. Nieves stares into Lupe's eyes and gently says, "You will never do such a thing will you, Lupe?"

"No," Lupe mutters. He is beginning to feel sick in his stomach. His mouth is dry.

"Again."

"No, Poppi, never again," Lupe manages to say.

"I am going to take you to the apartment, and you are going to bed. And you are going to stay in your room," Nieves decrees. He turned to Adela. "I'm sorry, Adela. I don't know why he did this."

Adela nervously smiles and looks at Lupe. She can see in Lupe's eyes why he did it. "It's okay, Nieves. I better go, I better go ..." and she disappears quickly, more afraid for herself in the well-lit barber shop than the unlit streets.

Later that night Lupe is lying in bed when he hears his father return to the apartment. Nieves goes into the kitchen and makes some coffee. Lupe hears him move down the hall to the living room, sit on the couch, and turn

on the television very low. Lupe pictures Nieves changing into his slippers and exchanging his smock for a
colored shirt. And Lupe listens to his father's movements
and waits for his father to come and say something to
him, but he does not.

Lupe is asleep when Nieves' voice awakes him.
"Poppi," Lupe slowly slurs in his daze, "I am sorry. But I
couldn't help myself. I had to scare her away. Adela is not
a good woman. I have seen her with other men. She sells
herself, Poppi. She sells herself to men. She wants you to
buy her. She wants to fool you and take what you have
left."

Nieves walks to the dresser and peers into the wall
mirror above it. In the mirror he can barely make out the
gray-haired sagging man he has become. "Can she take
you from me? Are not the father and son one, Lupe? Even
if a man and a woman gravitate towards one another like
a bullet to its target, father and son will always be one.
The blood is inseparable. The spirit is a single spirit
shared by two." In the darkness Nieves then smiles.
"After scaring Adela to death with that toy gun, I doubt
she will enter the shop again without checking to make
sure you are gone. Have you asked yourself, Lupe, what
a woman like Adela can give besides take? So many
lonely men must draw what little life they can from
talking to a woman much less sleeping with her. Look
what she can give back to an old and useless man like
me." Nieves reverses the proposition on his son and turns
away from the mirror to sit at the edge of his son's bed.

"You are not useless, Poppi."

"Ah, but sometimes I feel that way, you know,"
Nieves responds.

"You of all people are not useless," Lupe reacts.
"Everyone knows you. Everyone respects you. You are

Nieves the barber. I have watched you care for the men in the neighborhood. I have seen them kiss your hand, Poppi. Even the *tieres* do not dare rob you on the street. You have taught me everything, and someday soon I want to be like you. I will be a barber too."

"Is that what you really want, Lupe? To be a barber like me?"

"What is wrong with that, Poppi? Yours is a kind profession. How many times have I seen a man come into your shop and put himself in your hands then walk out almost feeling like a god, eyes bright, hair in place, manicured hands, clean-shaven or perfectly mustached. When they leave the shop, something about these men looks clear, pure, something that wasn't there at first."

"You surprise me. I thought you would seek something else."

Lupe reaches for his father's hand and holds it in the dark room. "Listen, Poppi. Listen. Listen," he tells the old barber, and for a minute they are silent. They can hear sounds all around them—the streets, the cars and trucks and taxi cabs and buses, the voices from windows and doors, the thumping from upstairs, the subtle rhythms of a city with perpetual insomnia. "This is the world, Poppi. The world is here in us, and we are in it. I don't have to go far to see everything that matters to me."

The silence between them continues. There is a distant music.

"What has made you so strangely wise?" Nieves finally states with bewilderment.

"You have," Lupe firmly answers. "The father and son are one. Your words, Poppi, your words. I have learned from you, from your good words and from your mistakes. Maybe it's time you force me out of being a boy. Like when your mother forced you and your brother Pedro from her house on the island long ago. I am not a boy anymore, my father."

*Chapter Seventeen*

## ROOM OF RUINED LIGHT

Cold days and the winter sky has an unusual light, dense and foggy like breath on the inside of a glass window. Quietly rising to the sky, the fire escapes are bare except for touches of snow piled on steps and settled on gratings. The buildings also wear the white drape from beneath which only shadows of shapes are rediscovered and not the things themselves.

Cold nights and the city disappears into a white hole where even voices get lost amid the banging of steam pipes. In the living room the television sparks like a fiery window Nieves can climb through to enter another room where old movies play out their stories all night long until dawn. Nieves shakes his head in the dark, not believing the image before him. Then he rises and walks down the hall to Lupe's room.

Gently, Nieves shakes his son awake. "Come with me. *The Late Late Movie* is on. Something remarkable, my boy. Something I have to show you." And he leads the boy who is half asleep to the living room illuminated only by the light of the television. Piano music is playing, and on the screen is the face of a stranger, a mysterious man in a turban. He is romancing a woman who cannot resist him, and the desert stretches to the horizon. The image intrigues the boy, and he sits with his father in the dark mystified by what he sees. "His name was Rudolph Valentino." Nieves lights a cigarette, inhales deeply, then exhales, the smoke suspended in the television's light. "I once cut his hair."

The love scene begins. "Who are you, my lord?" the intertitles read, for the fearful woman's lips move in silence. Valentino lights a cigarette, removes his robe and jewelled belt. "I am he who loves you. Is not that enough?" he responds. His face takes the screen, and his eyes widen and glow. Desert winds blow outside the tent heaving from the strength of the sandstorm to come.

It is quiet in the room. Both Nieves and his sixteen-year-old son are lit up by the glow of the television. Only music stirs around them and the commanding figure of Valentino on the screen. And Lupe stares deeply into the light-box and wonders what this man has to do with his father.

There is no smell of coffee the next morning. There is no sound from the kitchen. Lupe rises from his bed and calls out for his father. There is no response from Nieves who sleeps in the living room. Lupe puts on his special shoes and slowly limps down the hall. His leg always aches in the morning, especially cold mornings.

The old barber is lying on the couch. He is very still. Lupe shakes him and struggles to wake Nieves, whose mouth is open, a gurgling sound coming forth in an attempt to catch his breath.

*Chapter Eighteen*

## THE SNOWS OF JANUARY

The whisperers gather at Nieves' barber shop.

"The boy went mad, you know, when he found his father unconscious. He ran out into the hall shouting, falling and tripping over his own crooked leg."

"Mrs. Sanchez next door tried to calm him. She heard him banging on her door. She never realized he had such strength. He had tried to lift Nieves off the couch, to get him to sit up and breathe on his own, but Nieves was paralyzed, and there was a gurgling sound coming from his throat. His face had sagged, and he was sprawled half on the couch and half on the floor when Mrs. Sanchez came in."

"Poor Nieves," Mangual mumbles absently.

"The ambulance came screaming like a crazed girl to the front of the building, and Lupe got in the ambulance with Nieves, even though the men in the white suits weren't going to let him. He fought like a *muchacho* from the streets, told them angrily that this was his father and that they were not going to take the father without the son. When they saw he was crippled, the men in white didn't resist. And I'll be damned, they didn't stop Lupe then."

"I must quickly go to Nieves. I must see Lupe," Mangual repeats as if to himself but actually to the men who surround him with words.

"But wait, Mangual. There is more you need to know."

"There is no hope, Mangual. No hope for the old barber."

"A priest was called in to give Nieves the last rites. Father Santiago from St. Athanasius arrived and a small miracle happened."

"Very small and very strange."

"The old barber sat up and told the priest he would not confess to him. He would not confess, and he would not permit the last rites. He cursed the poor priest. Kept shouting that the father and the son were one and would not confess to the priest his past sins, would not ready himself to die a proper death."

"If there is such a thing, Mangual, as a proper death for any of us."

"Well, I don't know how all of you feel, but Father Santiago was mortified, horrified. He pulled back, the cross held before him. Nieves scared him terribly. I mean, here's a man almost dead, and he erupts with such viciousness at a man of the cloth."

"Eh, you take it too serious, *hombre*. It's just the old barber wanted to die in peace."

"Yeah, and Nieves is no hypocrite. Maybe he thought it was too late to make things right, *señores*, too late."

"Enough, enough, my friends," Mangual interrupts. "What happened after that? Did Nieves take the host? Did he confess?"

"Only if the roof of this shop caved in."

"No, no, no, of course, the old man did not confess."

"Absolutely. He's always been a man of his word, that I must say."

"No, instead Nieves collapsed back into his bed, breathing the last of earth's air. Then the priest, shaking like a black bug against a light bulb, stepped forward once again."

"Mangual, here's a priest who never gives up. We must send him all our lost causes, *muchachos*."

"*Silencio, hombre.* He goes forward again, cross in one hand, rosary beads in the other, and he began once more to prepare Nieves for confession. But the old barber motions with his one good arm towards his son Lupe. Then towards the door."

"It was very frightening. I almost went to my knees."

"Lupe had to ask Father Santiago to leave the room. His presence was upsetting his father, Lupe told the priest. The barber did not want the priest there in his last hours of life."

"And that's when we realized, Mangual, that Nieves wanted to speak to his son, not to the priest who had come to save Nieves' soul. The priest took his crucifix, beads, holy water, and bread and walked away, saying very privately to Lupe what he should do for his father."

"I heard those words, Mangual. I was standing closest to the priest."

"What did you hear, *hombre*. Tell us all."

"Father Santiago said to Lupe, 'Thou shalt wash him, and he shall be made whiter than snow.' And I looked to the window, and tears almost came to my eyes. *Muchachos*, that's when the snow began to fall again."

"*Oye, quécosa.*"

"And then, Mangual, Lupe began by washing his father's feet and his hands and his face, and at the end of the cleansing, he sat by his father, listening for any words Nieves was able to force from his lips. And then, Mangual, we left the room."

"Is this sacrilege? Have we witnessed sacrilege?"

"I do not know, my old friends." Mangual wipes his forehead.

"Ah, and one thing more, Mangual, for I saw this myself today. The boy seems to hear Nieves even if the old man does not speak."

"Yes, yes, I saw that too."

"Go to the hospital, Mangual. Go and you will see this mysterious thing that is happening. Lupe is sitting at Nieves' bedside. The old man is still and quiet as death itself, and the boy listens to the silence or something else we cannot hear."

"Something else we may not be privileged to hear, *señores*."

"The boy nods every few seconds. His lips move as if he were praying or repeating words to himself, repeating the phrases of comfort."

"It is not Nieves we feel sorry for right now. We feel sorry for Lupe. Grief lines his eyes. This sight would make a soul crack in agony. It is Lupe who we may also lose."

"Go now, Mangual. Tell us what is happening to the boy. He may not speak to us."

"But he will speak to you, Mangual."

"Tell us if Nieves will die. Tell us what message the boy carries."

Mangual droops through the dark streets cold with the new snow. The hospital lights flame ahead with their warmth. Even the buildings seem to shiver. But it isn't the buildings. It is Mangual who is shivering down to the bone, down to the last roar of blood in his very cold ears. Mangual, feeling very old for the first time, thinks about how his friend Nieves is dying and about how everything is like the snow, an icy illusion.

Mangual enters the hospital, its smells and its sounds. He feels dizzy and almost forgets why he has come. When he arrives at the ward where Nieves lies, he sees what he has been told he would see—Lupe frozen in his chair by the bed of the dying barber. Nieves' head is slightly propped up and looks larger than usual, serious, pale. Mangual stands nearby for a long time and observes what the whisperers have described. Lupe is staring at his father.

"Lupe," Mangual whispers. "Lupe," again.

The boy doesn't move. He is talking to himself but very silently, nearly unnoticeable. Lips moving irregularly, Lupe's voice is held within like a throaty whisper. He is deeply involved in some exchange, for there are words in him, but they are not his words. They are not Lupe's words but Nieves' words.

"Lupe," Mangual continues, "Lupe, I just heard. I would have been here sooner but ... "

Lupe raises his hand, a signal to Mangual that no explanation of delay is necessary. "He has been speaking to me," Lupe says. "He has been trying to clear his conscience. He has been trying to tell me everything that weighs heavy on him."

"Everything?" Mangual asks. Before Lupe answers Mangual continues. "Lupe, my friend, you look exhausted. How long have you sat here? Almost two days and two nights? Lupe, I am worried about you. Take a good look at yourself. You haven't eaten, you haven't slept. How can you help your father if you faint away from fatigue, if you collapse into tiredness. He needs you, but he needs you alive and well, not just barely alive or barely well."

"I cannot leave, I cannot leave," Lupe persists. "He has not finished unburdening his guilty soul. Something is truly on the tip of his tongue, something so terrible he wouldn't tell the priest. I cannot leave. I must find out what happened with the hair, the hair, Mangual. Valentino's hair. Do you know, do you know?" Lupe throws his head back. He is slumped in the chair. He closes his eyes in a lifeless revery.

"Lupe," Mangual softly whispers. The boy doesn't move, doesn't react. "Lupe," again Mangual gently calls. Mangual is suddenly seized by panic. The boy is not breathing. "Lupe, Lupe, come back," Mangual shouts again and again. The shadow of a nurse appears at the door.

Lupe opens his eyes. "I am so tired. So tired." He looks up at Mangual. "What do I do? Mangual, what do I do?" Lupe begins to sob, and Mangual reaches down and places his large hands on his shoulders. "Do you understand, Mangual? He is telling me everything I must know and everything he must tell before he is finally gone from this earth, before the ground opens for him. Do you understand, Mangual? You knew my father when he was very young. You knew a man I never saw. You saw him young, and you were with him longer than I could ever have the chance to be. If only sons could truly know their fathers. If only old age was not such a clever disguise to hide the secrets of a man's life." Lupe turns to observe the fading body of the barber.

"It's alright, it's alright," Mangual states for both Lupe and the nurse's sake. Her shape disappears from the door. "Lupe, you say he spoke to you. What do you mean he spoke to you? Hasn't he been unconscious?" Mangual once again scans his old friend's body. Nieves is at the edge of the waters of oblivion, he thinks to himself. How could this man so close to death speak to anyone? Mangual feels the tears dampen his cheeks. He resents his own weakness. He must be strong for the sake of his friend's only son. Mangual must not lose his courage now. He must wait until he is alone. Alone, he will howl at the moon. Alone, he will smoke his cigar and drink himself into listlessness. Alone, he will play the old fool and curse his isolation. "Lupe," Mangual begins again, "how did he speak to you? He's had a terrible stroke, and he cannot speak. He is not speaking. He cannot move. Lupe, he's paralyzed. And what did he tell you? What?"

Lupe stumbles with his explanation, for he is not sure himself. "I don't know, Mangual. All I know is that at first I listened very closely. His speech was slurred. And then like in a movie or on television, maybe, when you hear voices but see no lips moving, I could hear him, I could hear his voice telling me the things he has always wanted to tell me, to tell someone. Maybe he always wanted to tell me."

"Maybe, maybe," Mangual agrees, nodding his head.

Lupe surveys Mangual's face. The light from the hallway reveals the large bald head, the little hair growing along the sides and the back, the darkening whiskers, and the tear-filled eyes. "I am so sorry, Mangual. I have forgotten about how you must feel. We will both be very lonely without him. I know my father is dying. He knows he is dying. But, Mangual, he has not finished the telling, and I am so weary, so weary I can hardly understand him, I can hardly hear him," Lupe says with a mouth full of tears and his hands held tightly to his head.

Nieves squirms slightly in his bed, then gasps with the clumsy lips of a stricken man, "*Cuida el pelo ... el pelo*, Lupe," and rests back deeply into the pillow, into the white sheets, like a gray stone sleeping on the snow.

"Mangual," Lupe says as he faces his father. "Please help me. He will die soon, very soon. I must find the black leather box before someone else does. I must find it." Lupe drops his head down into his hands. "Please help me,

Mangual. It should be somewhere in the apartment. Maybe in the barber shop. But I must at least do this much." Lupe raises his head and reaches into his shirt. He pulls out the silver chain he wears around his neck. On the chain are three keys.

"We will do this then," Mangual agrees. "And, Lupe, you must get some sleep before you return to your father's side."

"And when we are done we must ask old Mario to prepare my father for the journey we all must make someday," Lupe says as he turns with new eyes to face his father's friend.

At first Lupe and Mangual walk silently through the snow. The snow is falling, falling slowly but heavily. Lupe thinks he can almost hear the snow thump gently, sounding like a million hearts beating, beating on the sidewalks covered with the delicate snow.

"My father did something with Valentino's hair. Didn't he, Mangual? Something that caused his great shame." Lupe waits for a response, but there is none. "It doesn't matter what it is, Mangual. It really doesn't matter. I will love him no matter what he did. But now I want to keep my father from burning in hell. That's all. I don't want to abandon him. Already his face is dissolving before me like this snow surrounding us." Lupe's bittersweet words graze the cold brick.

Mangual wishes he could swallow his own words, wishes he could keep himself from telling Lupe anything. They continue their slow walk through the snow. This night of Mangual's life is too cold. His false teeth begin to click together, and Lupe turns to see how old Mangual is chilled. He wraps his arms around Mangual in a gesture to somehow warm his father's closest friend.

"We will help your father rest in peace forever,

Lupe, or at least for the forever any of us may have left, for the forever you have left, my boy," Mangual tells Lupe as they approach the barber shop door.

The barber shop is still and dimly lit by a single fixture over the long mirror. Lupe searches his father's station and finds nothing. A quick search of the cabinets in the back room reveals nothing. The emptiness the two feel staggers before them when they both look into the long mirror and are shocked at their grim faces. In this light they appear to be drowning in dark water, their faces puffy, their eyes swollen.

In Nieves' apartment a chill persists. Mangual goes into the kitchen and begins to boil some water. He searches the shelves and finds some dried leaves. They make a soothing tea which helps with sleep and dreams, or so Nieves once told Mangual. Mangual measures two tablespoons into the boiling water then cuts off the fire to let the leaves simmer.

"No coffee, Mangual?" says Lupe from the kitchen entrance, surprising Mangual.

"This will help you, Lupe. It will help you sleep. Your father used it on nights when you were not here, when you would be at your mother's house, and he would be lonely for you. He told me it helped him dream good dreams. You would be in some of those dreams. And others that he loved, others who were now gone from him," Mangual explains. He looks down and notices Lupe has found the black leather case. "Wonderful. Where did you find it?"

"Where I last thought he put it—his coat pocket. There it was folded neatly over the chair in the living room, just as he left it the last night he worked." Lupe puts the small black leather box on the kitchen table. "I'll never forget the first time I saw this. It was at my mother's house. I couldn't resist opening this box. And now I open it for a second time." He unlatches the lid and before him are the silver barber shears, the silver rat-tail comb, and the shiny straight razor with the white pearl handle. All three rest on the faded red satin compartment. The other compartment has a glass lid which is slightly embossed with a wavy design, like the waves of hair. Lupe lifts this lid. There, sleeping in the far corner, snug in the satin, is a small pill box. His father's initials are on the silver pill box, the F.N. in a script with curly ends. Lupe holds his breath and opens the pill box. "Here is what remains of Valentino's hair," he announces and passes the box to Mangual.

Mangual holds the pill box close. His eyes are weaker than when he first saw the results of Facundo Nieves' first meeting with Valentino. There, clustered at the bottom of the pill box, are a few short clippings of black hair, enough perhaps to consist of a brief fingerprint identifying its owner. He holds this briefly in his hand, and then Mangual begins to weep. "Please, please. Here. Take this away from me. I cannot bear to look at the tools, at the hair." He turns to the stove and removes the steeping tea.

"I am so sorry, Mangual. I am so sorry," Lupe apologizes, his voice cracking from exhaustion. "I did not mean to cause you more pain."

Mangual wipes his eyes with the back of his hands. He strains the tea and pours a cup for Lupe. "Here, boy. Drink."

"What about you, Mangual?" Lupe asks. "Don't you need something to warm you?"

Mangual is searching the cupboard. "I have it right here," he answers. The rum bottle he finds has at least one drink in it. He uncorks it and drinks directly from the bottle. "Ah, that is good."

Lupe sips his tea and says nothing. His head hangs down, and his eyes are trained on the cloth covering the kitchen table. Each spot on the cloth is now a story. Each warp in the fabric has its own language. "I will stay here tonight, Mangual," Lupe finally says, interfering with the snowy silence which holds both of them. "I am home. You do not have to stay with me."

"Are you sure, Lupe? Are you sure? There is so much memory for you here. Are you sure you will not be lonely?"

"Yes, I am sure. I am very lucky. I did not know that until this moment. Everyone else is looking for himself. I have been lucky to always have a self right here. *Aquí*. Everything here speaks to me. My brothers and sisters of the imagination are here. My past, my future, they are here also. My most restful days and nights have been here. Here I have nothing to be afraid of. I step one way, I am a little boy. I step the other, I am a man. I look in the mirror, I see the old man I will be. The cracks in the walls and the ceilings are my children ready to break out and be born. It must be hell to not know yourself, to never know where your center is. So you see, Mangual, I am a lucky *muchacho* after all." Lupe places the pill box in its proper compartment. He strokes the barber tools. "I have always admired my father's tools and the tools of his hands. This is my true inheritance. Not just the barber shop or this apartment. My inheritance is that I am the son of Nieves the barber, the man who cut Rudolph Valentino's hair before his death." Lupe closes the lid of the black leather box. The leather grain is worn, but there are good years left. "You look tired, Mangual. Go home. I will be fine."

Mangual can see that Lupe is tired also. His eyes

are heavy, and he has difficulty with his speech. "Will you call me as soon as you are awake? We will go back to the hospital." Mangual glances at his watch. It is nearly two in the morning. "Of course, we may not have much sleep time left to us. Come. Let me get you into your bed. You look like you can hardly walk."

Lupe is weak. Sleep is quickly overtaking him. Sleep. Sleep. This is what he wants. "Mangual, I want to sleep in the living room. I want to sleep on the couch in the living room where my father sleeps." Mangual leads him into the living room, and Lupe collapses on the couch. "I am fine. Fine. I will just lay here for a while. I do not need to take off my clothes. I just need rest. Rest."

Mangual leaves the boy on the couch. He cuts off the lights. In the kitchen he rinses the coffee cup and places it in its proper place in the cupboard. Lupe is asleep when Mangual puts on his overcoat, pulls the collar up, and goes out the front door for the walk to his apartment on the other side of Southern Boulevard. The snow has stopped falling. Maybe the sun will make an appearance tomorrow. Maybe, Mangual thinks.

During the night Lupe lifts his head and sees light coming through the window which faces the back room of the barber shop. The light is subtle and gently reveals a figure seated in the chair by the window. "Mangual?" he calls out from his half dream, half sleep. "I told you to go home. I told you I would be alright. No need. No need," Lupe mutters. He lies back and puts his head back on the pillow.

The seated figure then speaks. "There is a fragrance to the sleeping, isn't there, Lupe? You know how it is when you walk into someone's bedroom early in the morning before the waking, and you can smell the sleeping body. Maybe you can smell sleep itself. And you

think that what you sense is dream or the convulsive
drowse of nightmare rippling through the body like a
storm of jagged lightning. Awake, Lupe, for I must speak
to you one last time."

*Chapter Nineteen*

## VALENTINO'S HAIR

I must let you know I have a stone lodged in my throat as I start to tell this part of my story, Lupe. It is a large stone I have wanted rolled away, I suppose like Jesus when he was ready to arise from the dead, becoming a spirit, and once again see the sky and the face of his father. It is a round and perfect stone meant to keep me silent, meant to gag me each time I dared to reveal how far I had gone with my wicked knowledge. This stone was my knowledge; it was what controlled my future and the future that was beyond my grave. So here and now I must roll it away.

Rudolph Valentino had died, and the night was filled with a light and gentle rain, almost a dew. And before me on this night was a most incredible sight, probably the strangest experience a man could have, to wade through a crowd of thousands grieving, grieving for the same person. And most of the people waiting outside the hospital were women, Lupe, wailing women. Old women, young women, Spanish women, American women, pretty women, ugly women, women with tired faces, women done in by their men, women in search of true love, women with children at their knees, childless women, women who looked like no more than children themselves.

The sidewalks all around the Polyclinic Hospital were cluttered with so many people that they flowed into the street and slowed down or stopped the traffic. Lupe,

I had not seen that since the end of the war, when we
marched home convinced we had fought the war to end
all wars. But instead there was dread and foreboding in
this night. Valentino's illness and death was not a good
sign to many. It was a sign of bad luck, misfortune, the
death of sensual love.

But it wasn't bad luck for me, I kept telling myself.
I was the man who cut Valentino's hair and learned of its
power. I was the man who had shaved Valentino in his
last hours. I knew him in a way no one else on that street
knew him. And Valentino had trusted me with the last
hours of his life. When the end came for him, he was alone
except for his three doctors and two nurses. He had lost
consciousness sometime after I saw him, and the doctors
had called in a priest to give him the last rites. He was a
priest from Valentino's little town in Italy. Yet the truth
is he had already received his last rites; he had received
the rites from me. The newspapers said that Valentino
did not know he would die. But the man I saw in that
hospital bed knew, knew he had little time left on this
earth. That's why he said *cuida el pelo*; that's how I knew
he was expecting me. The newspapers told about how to
the very end he talked about going fishing, about the little
boat waiting for him. And in the end he drifted off like a
little boat, drifted off to a cove somewhere on the isle of the
dead. That too I was sure of.

Lupe, it seemed like I waited for hours for Valentino's
body to be carried out. The news of Valentino's death had
spread quickly, and the crowds had grown beyond control. The police finally came in because the traffic had
been blocked between Eighth and Ninth Avenues on
West Fiftieth Street. I watched the anxious and the
curious as they were turned away from the hospital
entrance. I watched as they took on all kinds of decep-

tions to try to get into the hospital to see the body of
Rudolph Valentino. But the crowds were foolish. They
remained in front of the hospital, waiting, hoping in vain
to see the removal of the body. Yes, they were fools. You
see, my boy, I had been in that hospital only forty-eight
hours earlier. My body, my blood knew where he was and
how he would be brought out. And my blood was right.

The private entrance on West Fifty-First Street
was the only possible way for Valentino's body to be
carried out into the night air without the overwhelming
crowd swallowing up their hero. I made my way through
the weepers and the mourners and the shouters and the
moaners. I made my way along the building, staying in
the shadows as much as possible, feeling with my hands
along the building, a blind man using the touch of my
fingertips like divining rods. From the shadows I watched
the side door open.

One man stepped out into the street lights. Then
two men appeared, and they were carrying a wicker
basket with a golden cloth over the top. The first man
motioned to someone down the street, and from nowhere
a long black car backed up towards the private entrance.
I knew what the wicker basket contained. Valentino's
body. They were sneaking out his body to the waiting car.
Quickly, they lifted the basket into the back of the car and
drove off back down the street, away from where I stood
watching from the dark. I must have been insane, insane.
What makes men commit acts which are impossible to
justify with their everyday lives? With almost no hesitation, I began running after the big black car, running
as fast as I could. I had not run like this since I was a
soldier in boot camp, since running on shores of the beach
on my island. I felt the wind against my ears. The wind
whispered, *"Corre, corre, corre,"* and I ran, ran, ran, stay-

ing close to the buildings, staying within the shadows. My shoes slapped into the standing puddles, my pants legs were soaked, but my heart was pounding with a lurid joy.

I kept the car in my vision. The driver maintained a simple route with hardly any turns. The driver was obviously trying to not call any attention to the car or its occupants. He was careful, indeed, oh, very careful with its secret cargo. But not careful enough, for he did not see my shadow running like a wolf behind him or hear my shoes clicking like the claws of a wolf. And so the car went slowly for many blocks and stopped at Broadway and Sixty-Sixth Street. I was wet and shivering by then, but I felt like I could run on and on in the city's darkness. At the place where the car stopped was Campbell's Funeral Home. Of course, I thought to myself, fancy enough, big enough, and close enough. Hidden in the cavern of a nearby doorway, I watched them carry the basket into Campbell's. In a moment it was gone.

I walked closer to the plate glass windows of Campbell's. Closer. Closer. Until I was close enough to come face to face with my own reflection. Suddenly two other reflections joined me in the glass. Two men had quietly arrived and approached the front door. One of them looked at me and asked me if he was there. Quite simple, really. Was *he* there? Was Valentino there? I did not lie. The men looked frantic. The other man began knocking on the door. He would not stop knocking. The door rattled every time his large fist came against it. The first man told me that his friend was Valentino's cousin and that he hadn't seen Valentino in nearly five years. Camillo was Valentino's cousin's name. The man who spoke to me called himself Guido, I believe. Guido claimed to be a boyhood friend of Valentino. I did not question their explanation. After all, would they believe me if I told them who I was? I wonder. To this very day I wonder.

But I never had a chance to introduce myself to them. The door to the funeral parlor abruptly opened, and light poured down on the three of us standing there on the wet sidewalk. A man, a blond American man, opened the door. He looked very familiar, and he too caught my gaze and obviously recognized me. But he did not have the same reaction to Guido and Camillo who had immediately stepped past him into the lobby of the parlor.

The two Italians told their story to the American, and honestly, Lupe, they caused such a commotion that it was a miracle they were not picked up bodily by the security guards and pitched into the street. It was a miracle they did not wake the dead Valentino. The American nodded and nodded benevolently. The two Italians only wanted to view the body and pay respects. But the American very gently and considerately asked them to leave. And so they did with a little encouragement from the uniformed guards.

Then the American turned to me with a totally different expression on his face and introduced himself. I realized who he was. It was Valentino's secretary, the man who let me into Valentino's suite the day only one month prior, the day when I cut his hair in the hotel. I was rain-soaked, drenched, he told me, and he offered me a brandy to warm me up; to take away the grief of the moment, as he put it. We drank a glass together, in fact, two glasses in a private office just off the lobby area. I too came to pay my respects, I told him. He looked at me for the longest time. It was clear that he had not slept much. And I am sure it was obvious to him that I was under great stress. I began to tell him of the deep sorrow I felt.

I tried to speak, and suddenly, briefly, I lost my voice. It was as if my voice realized the futility of language.

The American then told me that he knew I had been in the hospital, he knew because Valentino had told him so, told him that Nieves the barber, that Nieves the man with the mother of innocent snow, Nieves the white angel had appeared to him, to Valentino, and all would be well. Valentino died peacefully, the American felt, because of my brief last visit. Without any warning, the glass broke in my hand. Just like that. The glass shattered in every direction, but I had only a small cut on my finger. Quickly, he took a silk handkerchief out of his coat pocket and wrapped it around my hand. The blood seemed to frighten him, and the cut looked more serious than it really was. But it was his kind gesture that struck me. "We do not want you to bleed to death, Mr. Nieves," he said to me. "After all, you have a funeral to attend." Valentino's body would not be ready for the private viewing until the morning. In the afternoon would begin the public viewing. Valentino's secretary gave me his business card with a note on the back which was the equivalent of a pass to the private viewing the next morning and the funeral soon to come.

The American walked me out into the lobby. There a woman was arguing with one of the guards. She was a pretty woman with very sad eyes. She was begging the guard to accept her offering, or rather the offering of her aged uncle, an antique dealer who had been a long and close friend of Valentino. In her nervous red hands she held a crucifix. It was more than a foot tall and was made out of nickel. It was inlaid with a tender design of flowers, forget-me-nots she said. She urged that, on behalf of her uncle, the crucifix be placed on the dead man's chest to protect him from evil. I was moved by her urgency, as was the American. He promised her that this would be done, and when I walked to the door, I could hear her sobbing gratefully.

I reached for the doorknob, but one of the guards seemed to snap to attention and begin to open the door for me. For the first time I took a good look at the uniform these men wore. These men were not security guards or policemen. They were dressed like soldiers. And they wore black shirts. They were wearing the black shirts of the Fascists, Lupe, Mussolini's Fascists. It seems that the Italian dictator had given direct orders for the American Fascist Party to guard the body of Rudolph Valentino. As the soldier clicked his heels, I stole out to the street where a crowd had already begun to gather.

A hysterical woman grabbed my arm and demanded that I tell her whether I had seen Valentino. Of course, I told her that I had not, which was true. She didn't believe me. She violently pulled at my cut hand, and I had to shove her away from me. Her attack had made the bleeding more severe. I rewrapped my hand with the silk handkerchief the American had used. Imagine my disbelief when I saw the initials on the handkerchief were R. V. With great speed I made my way past the gathering crowd and rushed off into the maze of streets. I felt dizzy. The people rushed by me. I was a stranger to them. We were strangers to each other, yet our bodies touched then parted.

The city fell into a deep darkness. I remember little of my walk. But somehow I came upon a small *bodega* on a sidestreet. It was still open at that time of night. The smell of *pernil* cooking drew me in. I ordered a pork sandwich, and while the man behind the counter prepared my order, I stared vacantly at the various bottles of herbs and spices on the shelves above his head. Two containers caught my attention. One was labeled *flor de cereza*. The other was labeled *raiz de ave del paraiso*. Cherry flower and root of bird-of-paradise. I did not wait for the man to wrap my sandwich. I was so hungry I sank my teeth into the sandwich while he gave me my change from the dollar I had given him. And as I chewed, I stared at the small bottles high above me. I chewed and I stared, and the more intense my chewing, the sharper my vision became until I was there inside those little bottles smelling the sweet scents of those beautiful flowers. "*¿Quiere algo más?*" the man said. Yes, I told him. Yes, I did want one thing more. And I bought the two small bottles which chimed gently in my pocket as I walked to my barber shop.

The front door of my shop closed behind me very severely, definitely, like the cover of a book revealing my life. And inside my shop I was to tell my own story. I rolled down the shades over the wide windows. Then I turned on the light over the sink and put the little bottles of powdered substances on the counter, next to the black leather case containing Valentino's hair. My hand was still bleeding, the cut still open and red. At that moment I remembered what the *bruja* had told me—to mix the ash of the hair with cherry flower and root of bird-of-paradise in a beverage of strong alcohol, perhaps rum would do, and to add the essential element, my own blood, my own blood.

In a shaving cream mug I squeezed my hand and collected the drops of my blood that flowed from the wound. They fell generously from the short but deep cut. Then I opened the two small bottles and added substantial portions of the lovely colored powders. Their aromas briefly rose and overtook me. I felt tired. I felt dizzy. Finally, I opened the black leather box and removed a good deal of the hair, enough to be effective, enough for a flask of rum perhaps, enough to bring the moon to my feet. Yes, that's what I wanted, the goddess of the moon to come to me. I put a match to the hair, collected the ashes, and added the ashes to the mixture in the shaving cream mug.

When I poured a couple of ounces of rum into the mug, I heard a sizzle, and foam rose to the top. It was effervescent, and a sweet gas grew in the air like a shiny or milky puff above the mug. The mix was ready. I poured it back into the flask which contained the rest of the rum, screwed on the cap, and shook it well. Then I hid it to the back of a drawer filled with folded clean towels. And in my exhaustion I leaned back in my barber chair and fell asleep.

I woke just before dawn. I thought I could smell the sweet scent of the potion still lingering in the shop. Quickly, I put a sign on the front door of the shop: Closed due to death in family. Very simple. Very direct. In the back room of my shop I always kept personal items like clothing and extra shoes, since my apartment was some distance. I washed as best as I could in the sink, and I shaved. My face was almost strange to me that morning. I was gaunt and pale. I had not rested although I slept, and the circles under my eyes showed this.

And as I shaved, I realized I had to be very careful, for my hands felt weak, particularly the hand that I had cut. I put a bandage on my finger and then proceeded to finish dressing. After putting on a white short-sleeved shirt and dark pleated pants, I put on a bow tie and slicked back my hair. Finally, I placed the wide-brimmed straw hat on my head, adjusting the angle of the hat so it dipped down slightly over my right eye. All the men in Nueva York were wearing these hats, even the Puerto

Ricans, for this showed sophistication, for this showed
worldliness. Yes, I could deceive that mirror I stood
before. I did look sophisticated and worldly. The mirror
told me so on that crucial morning.

The streets were still wet that morning, the sky
imposing and threatening with its dark clouds, so this
time I brought my umbrella. And I spoke to no one, Lupe,
no one. I walked in silence towards Campbell's Funeral
Home with only one purpose: to see Valentino in death,
to see the mask of death as he wore it. But it was also to
know that he was dead. To be sure. Is that not strange
how we do not accept or care to acknowledge our leaving
this world unless we see the dead, we see how hopeless
it is to battle the inescapable fate which awaits us. I had
to see him in his coffin. I had to know my grief, my
mourning was for some reason. If Valentino could taste
death, then I could taste it too.

When the front of Campbell's was in view, I knew
the day would not end without insanity, without hyste-
ria. Crowds had already gathered to view the body, the
line two abreast as far as the eye could see. But the front
door of Campbell's was at this time of the morning kept
clear for the friends of Valentino. The public would not be
permitted to see his body until the afternoon. As I
approached the front of Campbell's, two policemen on
horseback stopped me. One of the horses was deliberately brushed by me and almost knocked me down. The
officer on the horse was most insulting. "Where's the likes
of you think you're going?" he said viciously.

I was stunned. I hadn't been treated like that for
some time although Puerto Ricans in the city were not
welcome by most people. I pulled out the card I had been
given by Valentino's secretary. The second policeman
read the card and apologized for the first man's behavior.

It seemed that already the crowds were getting unruly and the police were beginning to feel the pressure. I asked him for my card, and at first I thought he wouldn't return it, but I stood my ground, and he did hand it back to me, waving me on to the front plate glass windows of Campbell's. As the door was opened for me to enter, I turned to see several mounted police charge into the milling crowd in the street. Women shrieked in terror while trying to scramble away from the horses' hooves. Their screams made my blood cold with fear for them.

Once inside, I felt safe from the violence which was increasing outside. I along with some others was led into the chapel whose entrance was guarded by the black-shirted Fascists, somber-faced and stiff. While I stood in line to enter, I recognized the mayor, Jimmy Walker, just three people ahead of me. He was with two other men who looked like city officials. No one spoke. We all just slowly took short steps forward into the chapel. Wordlessly, one by one, we came closer to where Valentino's body lay in this golden room. Before I realized it, I was close to the coffin-shaped structure covered with a pall. Some of us in line began to weep.

I heard one man begin a prayer. Four large bunches of roses were behind the massive coffin. Candles burned at the head and the foot of the silver bronze casket, and behind the roses were a crucifix and a small statue of the Virgin Mary. And there before me was the face I knew too well, pale and thin, eyes closed. He was dressed in formal evening attire. The lure of a gentle slumber, the pleasing love of eternal drowse now possessed Rudolph Valentino. Head slightly elevated, his black hair, slicked and combed back, was perfectly in place. The high forehead was smooth and white, no sign that worry ever occupied his thoughts. His lips were slightly reddened by the mortician's hand. What did his dark eyes see? I stopped and held my breath, held it to know the stillness the dead know. And then I began to breathe again and moved on to be led through a side door into the hallway and out a back exit. It passed so quickly, Lupe. Before I could gather my senses, I was outside on Sixty-Seventh Street where the traffic was stopped in its tracks. Across the street was a coffee shop where I went to try to recover. After being inside the funeral home, the moist air smelled wonderful, smelled alive. And for the first time in days, it felt good to be alive, it felt good to have my life back. The coffee shop was crowded, of course, but I managed not to faint from hunger before buying a cup of coffee and a danish.

All I heard around me was about Valentino. One man cursed him, one woman wept, others were there for the excitement. And as I stood pressed against the window drinking my coffee and finishing the last bite of danish, I looked out the glass window, and through the traffic and the thousands of curiosity seekers, I saw her.

I saw her, Lupe, I saw her. I caught her flash by across the street. I caught her left side when she briefly disappeared behind clusters of people. Then there she was again, dipping in and out between these irreverent mobs, between the children, between the entrapped automobiles. There she was. No, there. Yes, there and there. And I gave chase. I ran out into the crowded street, crashing into people, knocking some down, helping them up, apologizing to them, then moving on through the monstrous crowd, looking for the impossible. I knew she was there somewhere, and I was determined to find her. She was there for me, she was there for Valentino, she was there because today fate had brought us together.

I searched everywhere. I went from Sixty-Seventh

Street to Sixty-Eighth Street. There the police had thinned down the crowd to a single file, but that single file went south nearly two blocks back to the entrance of Campbell's. And people were constantly trying to break into the line from across the street, and the mounted police were constantly trying to hold back the crowd. I watched as several women fainted. At one point a man and his wife were ordered to get back in line or go to the back of the line, and that's when a tremendous scuffle began. When the mounted police approached the man, he suddenly waved his umbrella at them like a sword. Several police dismounted and arrested the man, but by then the crowd had surged forward, knocking me and many others down. One woman got hit in the head by a rearing horse. In the chaos I lost my hat. When I found it, it was crushed, trampled by the horses and the crowds, and my umbrella was gone, snatched out of my hand by some man quickly passing.

What must it be like to witness the end of the world? Does circumstance make cannibals of even the best men and women? Maybe so, my son. Maybe from the righteous comes evil and from evil comes the righteous. Maybe we are one in the same, and we keep trying to separate the two. I simply do not know. But that moment I went a little *loco*, you know. The crazy situation got the best of me, I must admit. I could smell blood, I could smell sweat and flesh. The next man who pushed me to the ground I would kill. Yes, that is how tormented I felt standing in the rain at Sixty-Eighth Street and Broadway. My only hope, my only salvation was to find her, the woman I was in love with, the woman who was not in love with me.

I decided to follow the line of thousands who were waiting to view Valentino's body. I began walking south down the street choked with traffic and virtually covered with people. Slowly, I made my way towards Campbell's. I scanned the crowds lined up on the sidewalks. I inspected each woman and watched for any sign of her among the gathered. And as I passed, each woman caught my glance, each woman seemed to begin to speak to me with her eyes or with her sway or with the way she crossed her arms or held her hands to her face. Each woman seemed to say, "Move on, Facundo Nieves, move on. Ahead she waits for you, and I am only here to send you away, to send you down this crowded river to where she awaits at the mouth of a channel you must swim to your island of destiny, to your island of lust." I followed these signs, these calls from the sirens who referred me to a farther coast of rock and violent ocean.

About half a block from the entrance to Campbell's and wedged between several loud young men, I saw a piece of the yellowish color I thought she was wearing when she passed the coffee shop. The men were boisterous and rude, quite unmannered and ungentlemanly, and when I approached, they took a very aggressive stance, trying to block my entry. I said, "Excuse me," but that did no good until I heard her voice from behind one of the bigger men. "Oh, there you are," she said. "I thought you'd never get here." Undoubtedly, she was relieved to see a familiar face, even if only my face. She told the men I was her boyfriend, and she had been waiting for me. They were not happy to listen to this excuse, but they stepped away and allowed me to stand in line with her, though they muttered obscenities under their breath. So there I was with her yet without her, for what love could happen in a place like this where the crowds were out of control.

Ah, what did we say to one another? I remember I was so relieved to find her, yet so nervous to be near her that now, as I tell you this, our words rush past like water gone downstream. She had been inside the gold room once already, she told me, but the funeral attendants hurried them along, hurried them so quickly she had fallen and scraped her knee. She raised the yellow skirt of her dress and showed me the bruise. I had to resist the sudden desire to fall down before her and kiss the cut there on her knee, to lick off the blood from the mark left on her, to taste her and know what I had hungered to know. Did it show on my face then? I wonder. She caught my look and smiled. Smiled. At that my heart sang, Lupe. I could hear an encouraging voice saying, "Yes, yes, this is the one who holds your life like you hold the razor, like you hold the comb." If I leave this world with nothing, I at least have that good memory to guide my boat towards eternity.

We had reached the front of Campbell's, and the rain had begun to fall again very gently. For five minutes a silence came over everything. Only the sound of horses' hooves and the shuffling of the slowly moving line could be heard. Then the silence was broken by a great wave of movement from the milling throngs in the street. An unexpected swell of shrieking women and surly men, their open umbrellas rising and rearing above us all like heavy black clouds, forced the mounted police to charge into the crowd. Without warning, the crowd pushed a line of policemen against the north plate glass window of the funeral home, and the window fell outward with a crash on the heads of the policemen and others trapped there.

Glass scattered everywhere cutting dozens of people caught near the falling glass. The frightened rushed away towards us, and she sprang into my arms seeking shelter in my embrace. I felt horror, and I felt passion. Here I held her close for the first time, but when I looked out across the gray street, I saw those who were scrambling to escape the oncoming horses, those who were limping away shoeless from the scene to nearby stores or to street cars, and those who were slashed and bleeding and trampled and screaming in agony. Because we were close to the entrance into Campbell's, with the group of people ahead of us and behind us, she and I managed to be driven into the funeral parlor. It felt as if we were carried by some great engine of humanity through the front doors, down a hallway, then up a short climb of stairs to a small room where Valentino's body had been moved since I had viewed his body in the morning.

In this commotion she clung to me, pressed against my heart. We were both tired and wet from the rain. I could smell a sweet rose cologne rising from her wet hair. Her skin felt cool and fresh. I had my arm around her waist. I pulled her close to me to shield her from the noisy and rude people around us. With my hand I could feel her hipbone. I imagined the curve of it and in my mind traveled that curve down her thigh and up again. I knew I wanted her. She held close to me, her cheek against my face, and she turned to me, her excited breathing touching me, skirting my ear. Then I said it. In fact, I said it as we stood no more than three or four feet from the casket. I whispered to her so no one could hear. I told her I cut Valentino's hair a month earlier. I told her how dismayed he looked at the time, how depressed he seemed. I told her I visited him in the hospital in his last hours. I told her I knew him well. I told her I had pieces of his hair. I offered her a piece. Her eyes gleamed. She put her hand on my face, on my left cheek, and held my face towards her. Yes, she said. That's all. Just yes.

We both looked down at Valentino, his face white and prominent, his lips touched with red, his shiny black hair, and I felt a sudden and deep sadness for him, for me.

She said, "Don't cry," and I realized tears were in my eyes. Once again she touched my face, touched the tears of my grief. Then we were hurried along and pushed out to another doorway and down another staircase leading to the street.

Outside, the world had gone mad. Ambulances were collecting the injured. The street was littered with debris—shoes, paper, bags, purses, broken glass, umbrellas. The rains persistently fell. I reached down and picked up an umbrella that was not yet trampled by the crowd and opened it over us. She told me she wanted to see Valentino's hair. She wanted to see what I had and to keep a piece for remembrance. Cutting through the insanity of people and police and garbage and chaos, we left this scene, walking silently in the rain until we arrived at my barber shop.

The shades were still drawn over the windows, and when we walked into the shop and closed the door behind us, we stood there and allowed the quiet darkness to surround us like the silent leaves of the rain forest depicted on the wallpaper of my shop. We walked to the counter, and for the first time, I saw her reflection in the mirror. Now I had two of her. She stood blond and radiant before the large oval mirror and smiled into it while actually smiling at me. She had never been in a barber shop, she said. She ran her hand along the counter, along the arms of the barber chair. She picked up the bottles of colognes and read their labels aloud. Watching her made me delirious. And then she asked to see the hair, Valentino's hair.

My black leather box was on the counter. I reached over, raised the lid, and revealed to her my tools. She touched the silver barber shears first, from the handle to the sharp point. Did I use these to cut Valentino's hair, she asked me. Yes, I told her. Then her fingers came to rest on the silver comb. And this is the comb used to comb Valentino's hair, she stated. Yes, I said. And finally she stopped at the straight razor with the pearl handle.

It is beautiful, she said. With this razor I gave Rudolph Valentino the last shave before his death, I told her. She was thrilled by this. May she pick it up, she asked. Of course, you may, I told her. Carefully, she brought it out of its place in the red satin bed. She held it to the light, allowing the single bulb above the counter to bounce a shine off of the perfectly unmarked blade. You can see yourself in it, she said. Was Valentino in pain when I shaved him, she asked, was he in his fever. Yes, very much so, I confirmed for her, but he was drugged and close to the end of his fight to live.

And he recognized you, she questioned, he knew you. Yes, indeed, I remarked, he knew me better than I knew myself. What did I mean by that, she questioned. I opened the glass lid of the other compartment in the black leather box and revealed to her the hair which was plentiful and almost to the brim. I told her that I suspected he knew all along I had saved his hair from that haircut a month prior. I told her of his last words to me—to take care of the hair, *cuida el pelo.*

Well, Lupe, she actually shivered with surprise and became cold. I noticed her nipples rose with this chill and became pronounced through the material of her yellow dress. She was wearing no brassiere, like many women of that day, probably just a lightweight slip to cover her beneath the dress of a late summer. May she touch it, she asked. Yes, of course, I responded. Gently, I took out a generous wisp of hair and placed it in the palm of her hand where she held it up to her like a baby bird. She put it to her lips and kissed it. Yes, Lupe, kissed the

hair. An emotion surged in me, rose to my mouth like bile.
I was jealous. Her lips were on his hair, its fragrance
rising into her nostrils like steam.
     And then she became dizzy. She put her other hand
up to her forehead and swooned into the barber chair,
falling back while carefully holding the hair like an
irreplaceable possession. She needs something to drink,
I said to her. Yes, yes, she mumbled, almost unlike
herself, yes, something to drink, for me to please bring
her something to drink. I brought out from the back of the
towel drawer the flask. Here, I said to her, handing her
one of two small glasses I had poured. Here, this will
bring back the color, this will warm you. May I keep this,
she asked me about the hair she held in her hand. I
nodded and drank the contents of my glass in one
swallow. She put the hair in the small pocket of her dress
and drank, first sipping as if she were testing the flavor.
It was evidently good, good enough for me to pour a
second drink for both of us, and we drank again. This time
she giggled, and her blue eyes brightened like gems. I
poured us a third drink.
     How would I explain what happened next to me,
Lupe? Is a man evil because desire drives him to the
unknown territories of the flesh? I have longed for these
answers all these years. All I know for sure is that I heard
this voice coming from inside me or around me. A voice
that was my voice but not my voice. It was almost as if I
could not be sure who was speaking, myself or another
self I had loosened through drink from my deepest part.
I stared at her and knew we both were drawn into the hot
circle of lust. She pronounced my name with a desire I
had never heard. She put out her hands to me. They were
warm to the touch. All the shiver, all the chill was gone.
She said my name again and again and drew me to her

where she sat in the barber chair. By pressing one lever, I tipped back the chair. The headrest went back, and the chair was now in a more prone position. I came over her and kissed her passionately. From somewhere within the voice rose, the voice vibrated.

"Take off your dress. Show me the scars we all carry. Take off your dress. Give me your skin. Let me kiss the opening to your soul. That's it. Let me help you unbutton and release this cloth caressing your skin. Let me be the cloth. I have come for you. Remove yourself from yourself. Now. Take off your slip. Let me kiss your breasts. Let me give you this blood hardening in my thighs. Let me place my spirit inside you. Like a veil, cover me, swallow me, make me the ghost that will haunt you forever. We are the forces of water and rock absorbed in the night. I am the moon in your mouth. You are the dark womb I drink. I am the wall. You are the mirror. You are in me. I am in you."

Naked, we made love in the barber chair, the leather squeaking with each thrust from my groin, with each suck from the sweet opening between her white hips. Our moans filled the shop. The bottles shook. The chair trembled. We couldn't stop. We wouldn't stop. We were slowly becoming one flesh, one beast bursting with appetite. She began to shout, to shout very loudly, a scream, a scream I still hear, a scream of insane joy and ecstasy. I tried to cover her mouth with my hand, then with my lips, my wet and hungry mouth over her mouth, but she kept rolling her head from side to side, shouting and shoving harder up against me. Then I realized what she was shouting. It was his name, his name. Valentino's name. Again and again and again. And I heard the strange voice return and rise from within me, answering her cry of desire. "Yes, yes, yes. Give me your hand. Give me your tongue. I am the handsome one. I am your lover. I have come for you. For you." There was no thought, no restraint in me. Just the pain of pleasure as we pounded faster and harder in that chair, that accursed chair.

It was then that the unspeakable happened. To this day I can still hear the snap, the sound when a clean break divides the two substances abruptly, permanently. Snap. God, a quick snap and my whole life became a nightmare. The sound startled me. I was still inside her, my eyes closed, my soul possessed by the force of the moment, when I realized she had stopped moving. I looked down at her lovely face, shining with passionate sweat, pink with new blood. Her head was back and slightly to the side. But she was very still. She was not the hungry woman. She was not the vigorous woman. I pulled away, and as I drew myself from within her, I felt her spasm, and I knew, I just knew she had lost consciousness from exhaustion.

The drink. Maybe the drink had affected her. Or perhaps she had some health problem I didn't know about. Perhaps she had these fainting spells often, and I wasn't aware of it. But maybe this was a gift granted by the hand of excessive love. She had swooned earlier at the touch, the smell of Valentino's hair. Why not? And why not awake her with more love? I stroked her hair and put my lips once again to her waxy skin gleaming in the available light. I whispered her name in her ear and, to my surprise, found myself once again infected by this lust, this thirst for more which I could not contain or control. I put my hand between her legs, found her open and welcoming, and once again entered her, slowly, gently, and began to deliver with great kindness my want, my love for her. She was moist and resilient and smooth, and this one last time I indulged deeply into her, unable to quench, unable to satisfy, but burning for her until I once again culminated in fullness and collapsed on top of her wet skin, my mouth on her left breast.

For that moment I too felt as if I would not revive. I kissed her nipple; I pressed against her breast. And then I felt fear. I listened. I heard nothing. My ear was against her left breast, and I heard nothing. Where was the excited pounding of her heart? Why was her heart silent? I turned my head and listened with my other ear. Nothing. Nothing. I picked up her arm and tried to find her pulse. Nothing. Nothing. I shook her by the shoulders, then shook harder and harder. Her head, leaning back, uncontrollably wagged. Her lips were parted in her last sign of desire. But gone was her heavy breathing, gone was her tongue licking her lips in temptation and approval.

I got down off the barber chair and lifted her up into my arms. Lifelessly, her head hung back, her full weight testing me. I placed her back in the chair and noticed how her head dropped back again in the headrest. I suppose that's when I realized what had happened. I realized the uselessness of the situation. In the passionate violence of our lovemaking, she had died, gone from me in one swift movement. What happened? What went wrong? Was the drink poisonous to her sweet body? Did her heart fail? Was her body so frail that it could not withstand this night?

Or was it something else brought on by the strange magic of the hair—something broken, some unknown flaw? But who would believe magic to blame for any of this? I stood there in disbelief, the odor of our sex filling my nostrils. And I broke down. I just broke down and began to weep, the kind of weeping one would hear from a man being tortured. And I did, I did want to torture myself. God damn me, I had done this to her. I could not blame anyone else. It was my act of lust, my act of hunger, my responsibility, no one else, not Valentino, not the *bruja*, not Mangual, not this innocent young American woman I had tricked, I had seduced.

It was my fault, and I wanted to suffer for it, I wanted to punish myself for this sin of gluttony, this unforgivable crime. I grabbed my testicles, and to my absolute horror, I discovered my penis was still erect and hard, still separately alive with its own craving. It wanted her. It. Not me, but it. The drink had not worn off, and my groin had continued to boil with desire. Oh, how the torment of wanting and abstaining can bring fever to the brain. And, my son, so it did to me. I glared down at her body trying to ward off the need which filled my mind with heat. My forehead, my neck, my chest broke out into sweat, and with my maleness in hand, a bloom, a colorful stamen, I spread like a great dark tree across her and placed in her my undenied flower, my senses enrapt in the force, in the push for her seed. With each insertion, my tears streamed forth, tears of unstoppable sorrow and tears of terrible pain, pain between my legs, pain of sexual desire so intense that when I finally died within her, the rush from her vagina felt like my own blood. Exhausted from weeping and from making love to her one last time, I rose, moaning with sorrow and shame, and I reached for my razor, wanting to die, wanting to mutilate myself, wanting to slit my dishonest and unworthy throat for not being able to reject the enticements of her body. As I lifted the razor and prepared to slice down quickly, I caught the reflection in the mirror of an insane man, his eyes red and mad, his face contorted like the mask of tragedy. Across this man's thighs were bloody lacerations. My God, what was I doing? I had mindlessly begun slashing myself.

What had I done? What had I done? I had not meant to kill this woman. It was all a mistake. A terrible mistake. I loved this woman. I wanted this woman more than anything. This city had been a grim place for me until the day I saw her beautiful face, until the day I saw her blond hair glow in the sun. I had to pull myself away from that razor, the razor I wanted so badly to punish me for my stupid self indulgence. I dropped the razor to the counter, where it slid into the sink, my blood on the blade.

For the longest time, I don't know how long, I crouched in the corner on the floor, naked and crying like a lost child. I wanted to bleed to death. Unfortunately, I didn't. The blood dried into ugly shapes on my thighs. I became very ill while squatting there and threw up several times on the floor. What had gone wrong? I literally lay in my own vomit having finally fallen asleep from anguish and weakness. When I awoke, her body was still there in the barber chair in the same position, only now she had begun to get cold, so terribly cold. It was not a nightmare, I thought, it had really happened.

I placed a customer's white drape over her. And I placed a white towel over her face. I couldn't bear to look at her. She was a dead rose, and I shook with fear when I turned to her, for her thorns were now eternally in me. Finally, after what seemed like hours and hours, I did the only thing I could do. I needed help desperately. I needed a friend, someone who would understand what had happened. I decided to call Mangual. He was the only man I could trust. He was my only real friend, and he knew, above all, that I was not a murderer. He was also the only man who knew about the powers of the hair.

On the phone I was hysterical. Everything I said to him sounded like a horror. Mangual would keep repeating, "*Quieto, hombre, quieto.* Quiet, man, quiet. Start again. Tell me again, man. Calm down, man." Oh, God, just to hear his voice brought me hope. He told me to dress her, and he would be right over. To be patient. He would do everything he could to be there as soon as possible. Mangual's last words were "Dress her. Dress her, you fool. Dress her, or you are a dead man." You see, Lupe, I didn't want to dress her. I didn't want to look upon that face, that lovely face of a woman I adored, a woman I had killed.

I removed the white cover, I removed the white towel, and I began to weep again, and while I wept, I began to very awkwardly put her clothes back on her. First, I wiped her and put her panties on her, the scent on them so clearly hers. Then the slip and the dress and the shoes. Waiting, I sat across from her, crouched on the floor, still naked, scarred, and half out of my mind and weeping.

About an hour later, Mangual arrived. But he was not alone. Two dark-skinned Puerto Ricans came with him. I thought he had betrayed me. I almost didn't let them in. Because my shop was in the hotel arcade, Mangual had to be as inconspicuous as possible. He whispered impatiently through the door, and at first I wouldn't answer. "*Pendejo*, open this door. I am trying to help you for God's sake," he kept whispering, so he wouldn't be heard in the lobby. I was reluctant and afraid. But I had no choice. I let the three men in. "Put your clothes on," Mangual said upon entering. Then he noticed my cuts. He turned pale. My appearance truly frightened him. I was naked and distraught, and my good friend knew this was not the time to interrogate me.

While I dressed, Mangual made it quite clear what was necessary. He told me he would not bother to introduce the Puerto Rican nationals who were with him because, as far as they were concerned, they never knew me, they never met me. He directed the two men to the small room in the back of my shop and gave them instructions to bring out a storage crate I had there. While Mangual inspected the body, I listened to the men removing the contents of the crate. Yes, she was beautiful, he told me. But, yes, she was now dead. No one would ever believe the circumstances. No one would ever believe it was an accident, a sexual moment gone wrong. No one would ever accept magic as the cause, for instead it would be declared witchcraft.

"You are a Puerto Rican, Nieves," Mangual said to me. "You are not welcome in Nueva York. You are an outsider. In the eyes of the Americans you just killed an American white woman, a white woman they would tell you, you never should have been with. What do you think they will do to you? They'll say you lured her here, Nieves. They'll say you sexually attacked her. They'll say you murdered her. You haven't got a chance, my friend. The gambler's odds would make you a dark horse, a long shot. Do you think you can beat those odds? You feel guilty, of course. I don't blame you, Nieves. But look what they do to immigrants, to foreigners like us. For Christ's sake, look what's happened to those two Italians, Sacco and Vanzetti. Take it from me, *hombre*, they're two dead men. And you will be too. They'll crucify you, Nieves, and they they'll cut your balls off and shove them down your throat to make sure you are dead."

I would soon find out how true Mangual's words would be—a year later Sacco and Vanzetti were executed. But on this day I was stubborn. I told Mangual that I believed there could be justice for me. After all, I was a respected barber. I was an honest man. And, yes, I too was an American because Puerto Rico was considered part of this country. The closing of the crate's lid and the snickers of the two strange Puerto Rican men cut my speech short. Mangual stared in my eyes. I thought he was going to begin crying. "Nieves, you are my best friend, and this...this is a violent country. Please...listen to me."

So what was I to do? Well, it seems that the only possibility was to make it look like suicide. "She was upset. She was depressed over Valentino's death," Mangual said. "Let's face it, Nieves. There have already been a few suicides. Why not? Why shouldn't this work?" I was appalled. Suicide for my lovely girl. I couldn't believe what Mangual was suggesting. This would devastate her family, her friends. I fought Mangual at every word. Well, Lupe, for the one and only time, Mangual slapped me. Slapped me hard too. "You're my friend, Nieves. I am not going to send you to your death. I will not have your death on my conscience. And that's exactly what will happen if you tell the truth. The truth doesn't work in this country if you're a Puerto Rican. You're trash. You're worse than trash. No one will believe you, Nieves. Even your own people will turn on you to protect themselves. Don't you understand that if you tell the truth, you will be the one committing suicide. You might as well finish what you started and take that razor and cut your throat here and now."

He was right, Lupe. He was so right. We placed her body in the crate. Mangual slipped a folded note into her pocket. The two men picked up the crate and disappeared out the barber shop door. Mangual stayed behind with me. He did not want us to be seen with the two men. Mangual had given them precise instructions and a generous wage to complete the task. I could not say anymore. I sat down on the barber chair and began to weep again. "Come on, Nieves," Mangual said. "Let us go into the hotel. We will have a drink or two at the bar. We will make noise and laugh. We will be seen by everyone. They will say look at those loud and crude Puerto Ricans. They will probably say cruel things about us. But they will place you and me at that bar at this time and not where that poor girl's body is going. Come. Wash up. Slap come cologne on your face. Let's get drunk. *Pronto, hombre.*"

Two days later the morning paper listed two suicides. Both women. Both because of the death of Rudolph Valentino. One was in London, England. A young actress who had known Valentino. She was found dead in the bedroom of her flat. She took poison. Left a long suicide letter. The police also found many photographs of Valentino. She had met Valentino while on holiday in Biarritz. There had been a rumor of romance.

The other suicide was in the bohemian section of Manhattan. Near Washington Square. A despondent young girl had apparently jumped from the top of an apartment building. In her pocket the police found a suicide note. Very simply written. "Valentino's dead. I cannot go on." But also in her pocket the police found something very strange. Pieces of black hair.

The police never learned what the hair meant or whose it was. Eventually, through friends, I was told of her death. I did not need to pretend to be shocked. Tears welled in my eyes. She was a lovely person, I told my friends, a lovely person. Such a pity, such a loss. And inside I was a destroyed man, destined to carry this guilt until I was an old man, destined to never really feel that kind of intense love again, destined to be cursed to never utter her name aloud.

I did not have the courage to go to her funeral. I wanted to. I wanted to very badly. I even took the street car to within a block of the funeral home where her body lay. But I couldn't do it. I knew I would fall apart, and her family would wonder why this Puerto Rican barber was so deeply moved by her passing and what did he know of her. Instead, I went to Rudolph Valentino's funeral. The funeral took place on a Monday, August 30th, just a week after his death, at St. Malachy's Church on Forty-Ninth Street. The funeral procession was dignified, nothing like the riots a few days before. The coffin was covered with roses, and the church was crowded with the invited guests. I sat to the back and saw them all—Houdini, Mary Pickford, Pola Negri, and others whose names were known in that day. Valentino's first wife, Jean Acker, sat to the front and collapsed in the middle of the service. Nurses were in attendance, and they appeared like angels out of nowhere to revive her. When the funeral march began at the close of the service, an old man in a pew near me fell to his knees and shouted, breaking the calm in the church, "Good-bye, Rudolph. Good-bye, my friend. I will never see you again." The nurse rushed to him with smelling salts. Good-bye, good-bye, I said in my heart. Good-bye, my lovely girl. I too will never see you again, I will never bring myself to the point of uttering your name. I dropped to my knees, weeping silently, and one of the angels appeared at my shoulder, gently touching me on my arm, and I turned to her and began sobbing in her lap.

Now, my boy, good-bye, good-bye. There's a little boat waiting for me. I hear the dew falling in the rain forest. I hear voices echoing in the dark cool coves. The earth smells like a good place. *Recuerdame*, Lupe. *Recuerdame*.

## Chapter Twenty

# EL MUNDO NUEVO

Before dawn a nurse's aide checks on the old barber who is dying on the second floor. But to her amazement Facundo Nieves is not in his bed. She searches the ward and, after scouring the first and third floors, returns to the night nurse in a panic. Over the rims of her wire-rimmed spectacles, the night nurse glares at the aide skeptically and decides to see for herself.

When she returns to the warm glow of her station, she picks up the phone. "Yes, he is gone," the night nurse says to the other party on the line. "Please come up as soon as you can to remove him. Thank you."

The aide is puzzled. "Is he there or isn't he?" she asks the night nurse.

"You need glasses more than I do," the night nurse sternly responds. "Of course, he is there. And he is already cool. He wasn't expected to make it through the night anyway. Well, I better inform the doctor, so he can break the news to the family. Go and cover his face," she adds, and she picks up the phone once more.

Lupe chooses his father's favorite suit, the wide-lapelled, dark blue pin-striped suit Nieves wears in early photographs. Then Lupe polishes his father's dress shoes. He washes and irons the white cotton shirt his father had given him; it looks much better on Nieves the barber than his son. He chooses socks and undergarments and then delivers these things to the neighborhood funeral home owned by the Rodriguez brothers, all of who were once

Nieves' customers. Old Mario goes to the funeral home, shaves his dead friend and trims his hair.

The whisperers arrive and leave gifts in the foyer outside the memorial chapel where the barber's body lies. Lupe arrives with Mangual and his mother Antonia. Antonia's husband Louie Toro follows with their son Pipo. Lupe's grandmother Sofia enters accompanied by her youngest daughter Miriam, who carries in her arms a sleeping child, the little boy whose father's identity she is unsure of. Nieves' daughter Barbara has made the journey alone from Ohio to bid farewell to her mysterious father. Nieves' one-armed brother Pedro also comes from afar, Nieves' beloved island, and whimpers through the ceremony. Mangual's employee Pancho, the former boxer, timidly comes in with his wife. She is pregnant, very large with child, and must stay off her feet, so she remains seated during the brief service, looking uncomfortable and sad. Yolanda Martinez and her parents arrive as the snow begins to fall again. She is wearing a simple leg brace now. She brushes the snow from her hair while she speaks to Lupe in the foyer.

When the priest begins the mass for the dead, Lupe notices a late-comer at the entrance to the chapel. He rises from his chair to welcome the lady dressed in black who hesitates from entering. It is Adela, the woman of the street, and her red eyes are a stark contrast to the black dress she wears. "I am sorry," she says to him. "Please, come in," he tells her, and he leads her to a seat. He swears she smells like roses.

The foyer, laden with flowers and bread and guava jellies and photographs and fruits and bottles of wine and rum, acquires a festive but respectful appearance on this day of the funeral service. After visitors view the body and attend Nieves' passage to the new world, they congregate in the foyer and warm themselves with a glass of wine or rum, break bread, and exchange stories about the barber who once cut Valentino's hair. Their voices become louder. They have good things to say. They sing songs from the island. Nieves would be pleased, Lupe thinks, that his funeral creates such a gathering of his people. They will miss him.

The attendants are closing the coffin lid in preparation for the drive to the cemetery when Lupe enters the quiet chapel and asks for a brief moment alone with his father. They acquiesce and leave by a side door.

Nieves could be easily mistaken for a sleeping man. His face is smooth and at peace. Lupe places his hand on his father's head, affectionately patting the gray hair. "You never failed me, my father. And now I will not fail you." Lupe pulls from his coat pocket the black leather box. "For you, Facundo Nieves, in either heaven or hell. *Cuida el pelo*, Poppi," he says as he hides the black leather box in a secret spot where neither sun nor moon can shine upon it, slips it into the dark safe place of his father's coat pocket.

# BIOGRAPHICAL SKETCH

Yvonne Veronica Sapia was born in New York City on April 10, 1946. Her family originally came from Puerto Rico. Sapia received a Bachelor of Arts from Florida Atlantic University, a Master of Arts from University of Florida, and a Doctor of Philosophy from Florida State University. She has been the recipient of an NEA fellowship and two fellowships from the Florida Arts Council. Primarily a poet, her work has appeared in numerous literary journals including *Alaska Quarterly Review, California Quarterly, Carolina Quarterly, Kansas Quarterly, New Orleans Review, Pacific Review, Partisan Review, Prairie Schooner, Southern Poetry Review, and Southern Review.* Sapia has published two collections of poetry, *The Fertile Crescent* (Anhinga Press, Tallahassee, 1983) and *Valentino's Hair* (Northeastern University Press, Boston, 1987), for which she received the prestigious Samuel French Morse Poetry Prize. Her poems have been included in the Norton anthology *New Worlds of Literature* (1989) and *The Best American Poetry 1989*, published by Macmillan. Sapia resides in Lake City, Florida.